Will You Be Made Whole

E. L. Ayala

Will You Be Made Whole

E. L. Ayala

Copyright © 2000
All Rights Reserved

Cover art designed by the artist Schofield

Schofield has never received any formal training, so he gives all thanks and praises to the Lord for his gift. He knows this is truly a gift, due to the fact that he's color-blind. Schofield has a variety of styles that developed over his fifteen years of drawing, painting and sculpting. Styles that cover a wide range of colors, textures, and materials. His favorite style is "Canvas Sculpture". This style is: Pleasing to the eye, the sense of touch, and is also thought provoking. This particular style of painting can't be duplicated or published by conventional methods.

Schofield chooses to keep 95% of his paintings "one of a kind". He feels that this gives him a personal relationship with the collectors of his works.

To learn more about the artist visit his website:
www.cv-art.com

HE COULD BE ...

He could be the man that asks you for your spare change
He could be the man that asks you for your help
He could be the man that has everything going for him
OR
The man that's having a long string of bad luck
The truth of the matter is, he could be a number of people
Doing a number of things
The doctor, thinking about the patient he lost
The officer that mistakenly fired upon an innocent man
The pastor praying for lost souls

HE COULD BE

The man that gives you that million dollar idea
The man that tells you about yourself
When everyone else is afraid to talk to you
OR
He could be a homeless person
That society wants to go away

HE COULD BE

The man that leads you to JESUS

HE COULD BE

A father, A brother, An uncle, or someone's best friend

HE COULD BE YOU

Schofield

Dedication

I dedicate this labor of love, this talent, this gift, and this anointing back to GOD.

Write the vision and make it plain upon tablets so that he may run who reads it.
Habakkuk 2:2

I'd also like to dedicate this vision to my mother Elizabeth.

A very special dedication to the memory of Markham L. Butler

When Jesus saw him lie, and knew that he had been now a long time in that case, he said unto him...

Will you be made whole?

John 5:6

Acknowledgements

Pastor Johnathan and Evangelist Toni Alvarado

The entire church family of Total Grace Christian Center
Decatur, Georgia

Dianne J. Hamilton
Steven Byrd
Nicole A. Jefferson
Patrice Shahid

The entire cast and crew of *Will You Be Made Whole?*
the stage play

Matthew Lee
Lee & Associates Consulting

Spencer G. Stephens
Web Master

Reginald Simpson
Performance Audio Engineering

Keith Bogle
New Vision Photography

Schofield and Creative Visions

Scripture references...NKJ Bible

1

Keith pulled his cap further down on his head and pushed himself forward in line as the bus began boarding for Chicago. He intentionally avoided looking directly at the other passengers as he walked down the aisle of the bus to find a seat. Although it was four days before Christmas the bus was not as crowded with holiday travelers as he'd expected it to be. His mind was racing. His heart was racing. All he could think about was leaving Atlanta and all of the horror behind him.

Keith found a seat in the very back of the bus and flopped down with his back to the window. He put his feet up in the seat so that no one would sit next to him as he pulled a Walkman from his tattered backpack and slapped in a tape. He pressed the play button and fell back against the window. As he sat there he began to bob his head back and forth to the driving beat of the music simultaneously taking note of his fellow travelers. There were several older people and a couple of single mothers with small children, a pregnant woman with her husband and a hand full of teenagers. This was all right, he thought, none of these people would suspect him. None of these people could possibly know that he was a runaway. He was safe here.

He sat with his knees pulled up to his chest tapping his feet, and using his fingers as drum sticks on the side of his thighs. By his demeanor you would never be able to tell that he had never traveled alone before, or that he had just killed someone.

Keith Patrick Coleman was tall for his age. He was 13 years old but he could have easily passed for 16 or 17. His eyes clearly showed the emotional and physical scars that he'd suffered over the most recent years of his life. His mannerisms gave way to that of a boy who was uncomfortable adjusting to his post pubescent body. Standing at a height of 5' 10" he wasn't necessarily clumsy, but he was visibly awkward. Keith blew through puberty just before he turned 13 with all the grace and ease of a Bull Moose. His copper toned skin was surprisingly acne free. His dark brow gave the impression that he was always in deep thought whether he was or not. You could see compassion in his eyes as well as the hurt that he tried in vain to conceal from others. His facial structure possessed a sensual quality. His full nose and lips completed the picture along with the peach fuzz that had cropped up above his upper lip over the last month. Keith was proud of that fuzz. His mother told him that it made him look more like his father. Keith thought so too. With his father's good looks Keith knew that he would never have trouble getting any girl that he wanted, that had already been proven. He closed his eyes and rested his head against the coolness of the window as he reminisced about Dianne, his 16-year-old paramour, who months before had brought him over the threshold from boyhood to manhood. He knew that he might not ever see her again once he made it to Chicago but his encounter with her had given him the kind of cockiness and arrogance that is the tell tale sign of lost innocence.

Keith's recollections were interrupted when a rather affable looking middle aged woman shook his knee and asked if she could sit down. Keith roused himself and looked around the bus again to see that the passengers had doubled since he'd boarded. It seemed that this trip was going to be as crowded as he thought it might be from the beginning.

The woman that sat next to him shuffled and squirmed trying to make herself comfortable. She pulled off her overcoat and threw it over the back of the seat. Keith watched her out of the corner of his eyes as she adjusted and re-adjusted in her seat. She apologized to him and the other passengers around them for making such a fuss. Everyone, including Keith, looked at her with an insincere smile that seemed to say, "no trouble at all," even though they couldn't wait for her to settle down.

Almost 20 minutes passed and the bus hadn't moved. "What was takin' so long?" Keith said to himself as he started to get nervous. He looked at his watch and then he glanced out the window toward the bus driver who was having a leisurely smoke. He was just about ready to knock on the window to try and get the bus driver's attention when he saw two policemen approach him. He slumped down in the seat and pulled the collar on his jacket up around his ears. Did they know? Were they here to arrest him? Was he about to be handcuffed, dragged off the bus, and locked away for the rest of his life?

"Well since we're going to be sitting together we may as well introduce ourselves," said the woman next to him. "I'm Elizabeth Goldberg, and you are?" Keith turned away from the window and looked at the woman with great intensity. She seemed friendly enough, he thought to himself, but could she be trusted? He removed his earphones and decided to take a chance. He extended his hand and responded, "My name is Ke...uh I mean Carl." He thought at the last minute that it would be best to forget all about Keith Coleman. The woman gave him an odd look and then a smile began to form in the corners of her mouth. "Nice to meet you Carl," she replied as she extended her hand to shake his. She then took a deep breath and leaned back. "We may as well get comfortable," she continued. "We've got a long ride ahead of us." The back of the bus wasn't the most pleasant place to have found a seat, what with the accessibility to the bathroom and all. Keith knew why he chose to be so far removed from the other passengers but he didn't understand why Elizabeth had.

The exchange he had with Elizabeth made him forget about the two policemen just a few feet away from him talking with the driver. When he looked back, the policemen were gone and the bus driver was boarding the bus. Keith closed his eyes and took a deep breath as a rush of relief flooded over him. "It's about time," he whispered as the roar of the engine began to ease his anxiety. Keith put his earphones back on and leaned back in his seat. He glanced over at Elizabeth who had pulled a book from her purse to read, and was adjusting her reading glasses on her nose. He took note of the book title *When God Doesn't Make Sense* and laughed to himself as he thought that GOD had never made sense to him.

"Good evening ladies and gentlemen," the bus driver announced over the intercom. "I'm George and I'll be your driver on this trip. We'll be pulling into Chattanooga in about two hours for our first stop. In the meantime you all sit back, relax, and try to make yourselves as comfortable as you can. Once again we'd like to thank you for choosing Greyhound for your holiday travel."

The sound of the driver's soothing voice comforted the passengers and especially Keith. He watched sullenly out the window as the bus pulled away from the station. All the things that had been familiar to him all his life were zipping by as the bus picked up speed. Goodbye Atlanta...Hello Chicago.

Despite himself Keith drifted off to sleep but the sound of the bus back firing startled him. He awoke to find sweat pouring down his back and seeping through the fabric of his denim shirt. His breathing was labored and he found it difficult to focus. In his head the back firing bus sounded like a gunshot. He'd seen the gun clearly in his dream. He saw himself holding it. The same gun that he'd used earlier that same evening to kill his stepfather. In his subconscious Keith was reliving the events of the day that lead to his running away. He remembered how he'd come home from school to find his mother and stepfather fighting. They were always fighting. Keith's biological father Ray was killed when he was 8 years old. Ray was accused of cheating in a card game, an argument ensued and Ray was shot in the head.

In the spring of 1985, shortly after his 10th birthday, Keith's mother Carla married his father's best friend Warren Jackson. Ray and Warren worked together at the GM plant in Doraville, Georgia. Warren was nothing like Ray however. Keith instantly hated him and wondered why his father had considered Warren a friend at all, let alone his best friend. Ray and Carla were only living together at the time of his murder. Although they often talked about marriage they never made the commitment. Keith knew the only reason Carla attached herself to Warren so quickly was because she liked having a man around and unlike with Ray, Carla was determined to make her union to Warren legitimate. Keith often heard his father tell his mother that she was *fine*, and in his eyes she was too. Carla owned and worked in her own hair salon and sometimes Keith would go by the salon after school to sweep the floor or take out the trash. It was during those times that he would hear the women and some of the men goad his mother into marriage. "Girl you betta' grab that man before he starts lookin' somewhere else," Vanessa, one of the stylist in the shop would say. "Warren is a good man honey, he's got a steady job, and he knows how to treat a woman. You don't want the same thing happenin' to him that happened to Ray do you? You betta' go on and make that move before I do," she continued as the rest of the shop chimed in with their affirmation.

What they didn't know was that Warren was a bully. Practically from the beginning he bullied Keith. Warren made sure that Keith knew that he wasn't going to allow him to get away with the things Ray had allowed when he was alive. Despite Carla's objections, Warren continually found reasons to beat Keith. If he didn't make up his bed, if he didn't take out the trash, if he got less than a 'C' on his report card, Warren beat him and justified it by making it sound like discipline. Warren's "discipline" of Keith was always accompanied by abusive language. He often cursed at him and called him out of his name, "sissy" was his favorite. Carla was never very vocal about Warren's handling of her son. She felt that Keith needed a father figure in his life so she accepted Warren's abuse toward him as stern parental guidance. Despite the fact that he loved her, feelings of contempt began to grow inside Keith toward his mother because of what she allowed Warren to do to him just so she could have a man in her bed. The abuse shifted shortly after Keith turned 12. Carla could have made enough money in the salon to support herself and her son without having Warren around but she was a lot better at doing hair than she was at managing financial matters. Carla looked to Warren to help her out when she found that she had more bills than she had money to pay them. He soon tired of the situation, and of her. Warren started sleeping around and not with just anyone. To ensure that he hurt Carla he started sleeping with the very vocal Vanessa from the salon. He never made any attempt to hide his indiscretion. He loved throwing it in Carla's face every chance he got. When she tried to leave Warren he spitefully reminded her of all the money he'd given her to help with the shop, and he told her that she would never leave him as long as she had a debt to pay.

Vanessa quit working at the salon shortly after her affair with Warren was exposed in a very public, very humiliating way. Warren walked into the salon on one of the busiest days of the week, Saturday morning. He sauntered past Carla's station as if she wasn't even there and headed toward Vanessa. The shop was full of customers waiting for their appointments and both Vanessa and Carla had customers in their respective chairs. Keith was there too doing his usual to help keep the place clean. Carla continued to work but found it hard not to notice that Warren had wrapped his arms around Vanessa, much to the discomfort and irritation of her elderly client. Warren started kissing Vanessa on the neck and telling her what he wanted to do to her as he tried to coax her into the back room. Vanessa just giggled foolishly as the rest of the salon patrons gawked shamelessly at their brazen display. Carla had had enough. She excused herself from her client, grabbed Warren by the arm and angrily pulled him away from Vanessa. She ordered him into the back room and slammed the door behind them. Despite the fact that the radio was playing in the background you could hear the sounds of a scuffle and the two of them yelling and screaming at each other. Some customers felt uncomfortable and abruptly left. Others sat and waited for the outcome like salivating dogs. A loud slap resounded through the shop followed by another and then the door to the back room opened and Warren came charging out. "Let's go!" he demanded angrily as he grabbed Vanessa by the arm. "Get your stuff and let's get out of here!" Vanessa grabbed her bag and quickly filled it with her personal belongings. Much to the surprise of her waiting clients, and the elderly lady sitting half permed in her chair, she left the shop. Keith watched Warren as he walked toward the door with the fierceness of an attacking lion. As Warren reached for the handle of the door Keith gripped the broom that he was holding and charged at him. Warren turned sharply as if he expected to be attacked. With one fluid motion he grabbed the broom with one hand and backhanded Keith in the mouth with the other. The customers and the operators in the shop gasped and held their breath as Keith's awkward body hurled backward over a chair and came down hard on the floor. Warren then gestured to Keith as if to be asking if he wanted more but Keith turned away. "I thought so!" Warren sneered as he left the shop. A few minutes later Carla emerged from the back room. She'd been crying and was visibly shaken but she summoned up enough dignity to continue business as usual. Keith's pride too had been hurt. After he picked himself up from the floor and dusted himself off he looked at his mother as if he wanted to comfort her but instead he too left the shop.

From that day on the cycle of break up and make up continued between Warren and Carla. He actually moved out of the house for a while and stayed with Vanessa until he fought with her and went slithering back to Carla. It made no sense to Keith so he began to stay away from the house more when Warren came around. Most of the time Keith stayed with his friend Tommy, he also spent allot of time with Dianne.

Around 2:00 in the afternoon, the day that Keith ran away, Carla called him and asked him to come home, she said she had something to tell him. Carla discovered that she was pregnant and she intended to use her condition as leverage to force Warren to leave Vanessa for good. When Keith got home it was about 4:30. As he stepped onto the porch he heard Carla and Warren fighting again. He heard her screaming and he heard the sound of breaking glass. Keith rushed into the house and found Warren straddled atop his mother trying to revive her. Warren had slapped Carla with such force that she lost her balance and fell headfirst into the edge of the dining room table. "LEAVE HER ALONE!" Keith screamed. "GET OFF OF HER AND LEAVE HER ALONE!"

"Get out of here you little sissy!" Warren yelled back. Keith ran into the adjoining room and retrieved the gun that his mother had purchased years before for protection. He ran back into the dining room, took aim, and fired. The first bullet hit Warren in his left shoulder and caused him to stagger as he turned and charged toward Keith. Keith was terrified as he thought of what Warren would do to him if he got his hands on him so he unloaded the rest of the bullets in the gun into Warren's body. The gun was empty but Keith continued to squeeze the trigger. The clicking sound in the chamber was like a release in Keith's spirit. Warren lay dead just inches away from where Keith stood and when he looked up and saw that his mother had not moved he dropped the gun and ran to her aid. It was too late. The blow she suffered was a fatal one. Keith gently cradled his mother's head and cried.

Only moments had passed when he came to himself and realized that there was nothing he could do except run. Warren was dead, his mother was dead, and the police were going to be looking for someone to blame. He carefully laid his mother's head on the carpeted floor and kissed her lightly on the cheek. As he wiped his tears with the back of his hand he saw that he was smearing her blood on his face. Horrified he jumped up and ran to the bathroom and frantically washed his face and hands. He then ran to his bedroom and changed out of his blood stained shirt. He stuffed the shirt under the mattress of his bed and grabbed an old duffel bag that his father had given him from his old army days. He became robotic as he emptied his dresser drawers into the bag. He wasn't thinking clearly. He wasn't thinking at all. All he knew was that he had to run. He felt that he wouldn't be able to stay in Atlanta but if he could get to his

Aunt Gloria in Chicago, she would help him. She never liked Warren. In fact it was Carla's union with Warren that kept the two sisters at odds with each other.

He knew he was going to need money so he ran to his mother's bedroom and rummaged through her purse. He only found $50 and some change, he had to have more. He ran back into the dining room and reluctantly rolled Warren's body over. He found $225 in cash in Warren's wallet and an uncashed payroll check. He wadded up the cash and stuffed it into the pocket of his jeans. As he pondered whether or not to take the check he heard police sirens in the distance. Panic and adrenaline coursed through his body as he grabbed his backpack and the duffel bag and bolted through the backdoor of the house toward the nearest Marta transit station.

"Carl...Carl wake up." Elizabeth Goldberg gently shook Keith to wake him and inform him that they were in Chattanooga. Keith jumped up wildly and startled Elizabeth who explained that she only woke him up so that he could stretch or get something to eat if he wanted to. Keith simply turned away from her and stared blankly out the window at the cold gray night sky of Chattanooga. Tears formed in his eyes as the enormity of what he'd done began to sink in for the first time.

2

There was a 25-minute stop in Chattanooga and most of the passengers took the opportunity to eat dinner or to buy things in the souvenir shop. A few of them stayed aboard the bus and continued to sleep. Keith grabbed a burger, some fries, and a soda, and quickly got back on the bus. He purposely stayed clear of everybody; he didn't want to take the chance of being recognized later. Since it was cold no one thought it strange that he kept his cap pulled down over his eyes and the collar to his jacket pulled up. He devoured the burger and fries as if he had not eaten in days, and then he leaned back in his seat and waited for the rest of the passengers to board so that their journey could continue.

As he sat there he noticed Elizabeth's book lying in her seat. "*When God Doesn't Make Sense* by James Dobson," he whispered to himself. He then opened the book and read what was written on the inside of the cover.

"*Liz sometimes GOD doesn't make sense to us, but I know that everything you went through this past year is working together for your good. GOD is sovereign and He works all things according to His perfect will. You will get through this...Love J.*"

Reading those words made Keith curious. What had this woman gone through? What did *sovereign* mean? Why does GOD let bad things happen to people? Who was J? Keith looked up and saw Elizabeth pressing her way down the aisle. He quickly closed the book and tossed it over into her seat. Elizabeth noticed that her bookmark had slipped when she sat down. A knowing smile formed on her lips and made her entire face light up. "If you'd like to read my book Carl you can," she said looking at him tenderly. Keith flushed with embarrassment and stammered an apology. Elizabeth quietly assured him that it was all right and accepted his apology. She then put on her reading glasses and opened the book to the page she had marked. "What does *sovereign* mean?" Keith blurted out not looking at her. Elizabeth paused for a few seconds and removed her glasses. Her brow furrowed as she pursed her lips and searched her mind for the best way to answer Keith's question. *"Sovereign,"* Elizabeth began tentatively. *"Sovereign* is who GOD is. He is the Supreme Being over all the earth and all of us. GOD knows everything about everyone of us because He made us. He is king!"

"A king?" Keith repeated. "Like in England?"

"He is greater than any earthly king," Elizabeth continued. "He is king of all kings. And He can do what He wants to do when He wants to do it, and that is what makes Him sovereign... Carl... Do you believe in GOD?"

"I don't know," Keith responded. "I ain't never seen Him."

"Have you ever seen the wind?" Elizabeth countered.

"No," Keith thoughtfully replied.

"But you believe it's there, don't you?" Elizabeth questioned as she smiled and winked at Keith and then returned to her book.

Keith sat there in a quandary as the bus revved up again and pulled away from the stop. He wanted to continue talking to Elizabeth. He wanted to know if the things that had happened to him were GOD's will. But most of all he didn't want to go back to sleep. He didn't want to dream again. He wanted to forget. The words he read on the inside jacket of Elizabeth's book kept playing over and over in his head, *"you will get through this,"* but he wondered if he ever would.

A few hours later Keith was still fighting sleep. He switched seats with Elizabeth so that she could get more comfortable and get some sleep. It was nearly three in the morning, with the exception of the motoring bus all was quiet. He had listened to as much music as he could stand by then and had put his Walkman away. He looked up the aisle a couple of rows and he watched intently as a young woman nursed her baby. When she discovered that he'd been watching her she scowled at him, covered herself, and turned away.

With nothing but his thoughts to keep him company, Keith wondered what he would do once he made it to Chicago. He figured that his aunt would probably know about what had happened with his mother by the time he got there, and if she knew about it then the police would not be far behind. For all he knew they were probably already on his trail. He thought about his fellow travelers and how many of them might be able to recognize him if they saw his picture in the papers or on the television news. He looked over at Elizabeth as she slept and began to question why she'd been so nice to him. He became paranoid as he imagined her turning him in once the bus reached its destination. Even if he was justified in what he'd done, he still ran. He was scared and he ran. And now he was trapped on a bus with 65 strangers headed for Chicago.

"O.K.," Keith said to himself, "...you gotta think. What are my options?" He was paralyzed with fear. He knew that he couldn't go to prison. Because of all the prison movies he had seen in his lifetime, he knew that he'd never survive. His father was locked up once for about six months. "Jail ain't no place for a black man," Keith remembered him saying. Finally Keith decided that he would get off the bus at the next stop and not get back on. He would keep running if he had to but he was determined not to get caught. *"You will get through this,"* was the last thought Keith had before he finally gave in to exhaustion and fell asleep again.

3

"Hey! Hey young man! Young man wake up. You're in Chicago!"

Keith opened his eyes and looked up directly into the bus driver's face. George had apparently been trying to wake Keith for several minutes. Keith stretched his long body out and repeated in slurred speech "Chicago?" Then as if someone had thrown a bucket of cold water on him he sat straight up. "CHICAGO!" he yelled in a panic. He looked around to see that with the exception of the bus driver the bus was empty. At some point Elizabeth had managed to switch seats with him again although he couldn't remember when. "You gotta get off the bus now," George prodded. Keith sluggishly grabbed his tattered backpack from the floor as he rubbed the sleep from his eyes. When he picked up the backpack a book fell out. It was Elizabeth's book *When God Doesn't Make Sense*. He stared at the cover for a half a second and then he opened it to the inside jacket. The writing that he had seen before was crossed out and underneath Elizabeth had penned, *"Carl, open your heart and you will discover that GOD is all around you. He may not always make sense to you, but He will always be sovereign. I trust that when you read this book it will open up your mind...Take care of yourself, Liz."*

"Hey kid!" George yelled from the front of the bus. Keith looked up, saw the expression on George's face, and knew that he shouldn't procrastinate any longer. He stuffed the book into his backpack, swung it over his shoulder, and hurried off the bus to retrieve his duffel bag. "Man its cold! Look at all this snow!" Keith marveled as he struggled to balance his backpack and duffel bag. From the moment he stepped off the bus Keith realized how Chicago came to be known as "the windy city." Chicago winters were not like the winters he'd experienced in Atlanta. He was not prepared to face that kind of cold, nor was he appropriately dressed for it. "This is going to take some gettin' use to!" he proclaimed as he walked into the bus terminal. "I'm gonna need a heavier coat!"

Once he got inside the terminal he searched the crowd for any signs of Elizabeth but she was nowhere in sight. He made his way over to the pay phones, dug a quarter from the pocket of his jeans and dialed his aunt's house.

"Hello," came a shaky female voice on the other end. Keith could detect that it was his aunt's voice. He also sensed that she'd been crying. "She must've found out," he concluded. "Hello," she said again. "Keith...Keith honey is that you?" With a knot in his throat he slammed down the phone receiver and headed into the bathroom.

Keith braced himself on the edge of a sink and stared at his image in the mirror. What was he going to do? Where was he going to go? The police were probably sitting right there in his aunt's house waiting for him to show up. Keith was so engrossed in his thoughts that he didn't notice that three guys had come into the bathroom behind him.

"Hey baby what's yo' name?" Rico, the obvious leader questioned as he sauntered over to Keith. Without waiting for a response Rico grabbed Keith and swung him around. He was as tall as Keith but more muscular. "Did you hear me sweet heart!" he said menacingly. Keith shifted his eyes to the other two and noticed their size as well. He could tell that they were older than he was. Two black, one Hispanic. They also looked like gang members. At least what he thought gang members looked like according to what he'd seen in Atlanta and on television. "Hey man are you deaf or somethin'?" the Hispanic yelled through a thick accent. "Javier! Chill man. I got this!" Rico assured as he pushed the Hispanic away and collared Keith. Rico got so close that Keith could feel the whiskers of his beard.

"Get off me man!" Keith hissed through clenched teeth trying to sound as menacing as his attackers. "C'mon Rico let's do this punk so we can get out of here!" one of the other guys yelled nervously causing Rico to turn to him.

"Yo Q, shut up man and just keep an eye on the door!" Rico ordered. He then turned back to Keith. "Gimme yo' money!" he demanded.

"I ain't got no money!" Keith countered.

"You ain't got no money!" Rico said raising his voice in octaves to show his intensity. "You ain't got no money! We saw you get off that bus, man. We know you ain't ridin' without no money!"

Angry and frustrated Rico punched Keith in the stomach causing him to double over. The wind was knocked out of him and he tried gasping for air but Rico didn't stop. He pulled Keith's head up by his hair and slammed it into the tiled wall. Rico continued punching Keith in the face and chest with the force and power of a championship boxer. Keith tried to fight Rico off but he was no match for him. Rico put Keith into a headlock and with a running start rammed his head into the porcelain sink. Blood spurted from the gash in Keith's head and he fell to the floor. Rico rummaged through Keith's pockets and pulled out the remainder of his money. "Let's get outta here!" yelled Javier as he grabbed Keith's duffel bag and backpack and ran out the door closely followed by Q. Rico administered one final kick to Keith's ribcage before he too turned and ran out the door.

Keith lay whimpering on the floor writhing in agony as blood oozed from his mouth and head. It only took a minute for someone to come into the bathroom to investigate the source of the commotion. The stranger immediately called for help and tried to tend to Keith's injuries as best he could while he waited. Blood clotted around Keith's eyes and they started to swell. The bruises and cuts that covered his face made him unrecognizable. "Can you talk?" inquired the stranger. "Can you tell me your name?"

Keith wheezed and coughed and choked as he whispered, "You will get through this."

Drake Sommersbee, the stranger that found Keith after the brutal attack took an immediate interest in his well being. Keith's identity remained a mystery that he was unable to clear up so he was taken to County General, a hospital usually reserved for those with low income and the uninsured.

The news of what happened in Atlanta had reached the Chicago papers along with a picture and description of Keith. The papers read that the police wanted to question him in connection to the murders of Warren and Carla Jackson. Because of his wounds and bruises no one was able to recognize this comatose beating victim as Keith Coleman. That coupled with the fact that Drake Sommersbee claimed Keith as his son gave the hospital staff little reason to suspect that Keith was the one the police were looking for.

By Christmas Day Keith had still not fully regained consciousness. To keep up the pretense Drake put a small Christmas tree in the room that Keith shared with two other patients. It wasn't until the day after Christmas that Keith began to show some signs of life. He opened his eyes, at least the eye that wasn't covered with a bandage, and attempted to identify his surroundings.

"Hey son!" Drake whispered moving close to Keith. "Welcome back!"

Keith was disoriented from the drugs in his system still he tried to question what he was hearing. "Don't try to talk. Just listen." Drake whispered. "I found you in the bathroom at the bus terminal. You'd been beaten up. Do you remember that?" Keith nodded his head slightly in response. "These doctors and nurses around here believe that you're my son." Drake continued. "My name is Drake. I want to help you. I think you're in some kind of trouble, am I right?" Keith reluctantly nodded again in response to Drake's questions. He wasn't sure what this stranger was up to but he felt he had nothing to lose by going along with him. "I'm going to protect you and I'm going to get you out of here. You'll have to trust me, alright?" Drake said finally as Keith nodded.

From the time he pulled the trigger and killed his stepfather Keith began to lose control of his life and everything that was happening around him. As he lay recuperating in the hospital he wondered if he should just turn himself in and be done with it. But then he thought that his freedom was the only thing he could control. Everything he had in the world was gone. All his clothes, all his music, and $87.47. He had nowhere to turn and no one to trust but this stranger that found him bleeding to death on the bathroom floor in the Greyhound bus station.

In many ways Drake reminded Keith of his biological father. He had the same build and same coloring. He even had the same curly black hair. Oddly Keith felt that he could trust him. Drake Sommersbee...Good Samaritan.

As his wounds healed Keith became more recognizable. He felt that the time had come to tell Drake the whole story. Drake listened intently and then he went into action. He rounded up a couple of his associates and they took Keith out of the hospital in the middle of the night. Drake was the type of man who always had an angle. He hoped that he'd gotten Keith out of the hospital before anyone could identify him. But even if they did realize who he was he had never given the hospital a valid address so he knew that they would be hard pressed to find him. Drake was a man of many talents, and just as many identities. The hospital staff knew him only as David Slaughter. In a way this gave Keith a real kick because he had made yet another escape, hiding in plain sight, right up under their noses.

While Keith continued to heal over the next several weeks Drake went out of his way to help him adjust to his new life. He bought him all new clothes, all new music CD's, and gave him the run of his Lakeshore Drive apartment. "I'm not calling you Keith anymore" Drake announced one morning as they ate breakfast. "From now on it's K.C. got that?" Keith, or K.C., agreed whole-heartedly. He was more than willing to forget about Atlanta and the horrible nightmares that plagued him after the beating. Being known only as K.C. was just fine with him.

4

It had been almost a year since her twin brother, Kyle, died of a drug overdose. Looking out her bedroom window at the rain-drenched streets Katy's pale blue eyes seemed transfixed on memories of the events that lead up to his death. It seemed to her that nothing had been the same in her life after that. Her mother, who had always seemed mildly neurotic, became totally unhinged. The thought that her only son chose to escape the family in such a way was more than she was prepared to handle, and no amount of counseling was going to help put this family back together.

Katherine, Katy's mother, blamed her husband for pushing her son to commit suicide. It seemed that Kyle Jr., no matter what he did, would never measure up to the kind of man that his father thought he should be. Try as he might, Kyle was never able to come to terms with the thing that his father hated the most. "No son of mine is going to be a homosexual!" Kyle Sr. would yell at his son repeatedly. "You're a man do you understand me! If I had wanted another daughter I would have had one! I can not love you as long as you persist in this kind of deviant behavior!"

Kyle Jennings, Sr. was an attorney for the prestigious firm of Whitlow and Bates in Youngstown, Ohio. At 45 years of age he was just about to make senior partner and he wasn't about to stand still and let his 14-year-old "gay" son ruin his chances. Kyle Sr. felt that he was opening the door for his future as well as that of his son.

Katy and Kyle, fraternal twins, shared a special relationship. Katy, the older of the two, had a biting sarcasm that was always lurking just below the surface waiting for it's next victim. Kyle was the only one who either understood or appreciated his sister's off color sense of humor. There were several occasions as they grew up in the suburb of Canfield, that Katy would do or say things just to shock her mother. There was the time when they had gone to the grocery store and Katy began to fill the shopping cart with condoms. "Katy! What on earth do you think you're doing?" Katherine would whisper embarrassed that other people in the store had seen. "They're for Kyle," Katy would say. "You don't want him to die or anything do you?" The blood would seemingly drain from Katherine's already delicate complexion when Katy would act in such a manner. The more Katherine reacted the more Katy acted out, and Kyle loved it. Driving their parents crazy seemed to be the highlight of their young lives. Katherine's therapy was frequently the topic of conversation for Katy when they had guest for dinner.

Unlike Kyle, however, Katy was a loner. She was often found sitting alone in her room reading or peering out the window, watching, as the world paraded by. "There's gotta be some excitement out there somewhere," she sighed.

Kyle was as outgoing as Katy was cynical. However, the older they got the farther apart their interests grew. Right around their 9th birthday, Kyle's sexual interest began to peak. Unbeknownst to his father at the time, his first encounter was with the son of a colleague. It started out as a *"you show me yours...I'll show you mine"* game, and ended up becoming a lot more intense. Katherine, unfortunately, was the one that discovered her son's dalliance. That discovery was to become the beginning of the end for her family, as she knew it.

Katy was always protecting Kyle. Not only had she known that her brother was *"different,"* she accepted it. Her parents, on the other hand, could not. Katherine always did what Katherine did best, bury her head in the sand and hope that he would *"grow out of it"*. Her therapist advised her to "ride it out" assuring her that it was only a phase. But it wasn't a phase, Kyle protested vehemently; it was who he was. To spite his son, Kyle Sr. focused all of his attention on Katy. It had been his habit to bring things home for both of them when he traveled on business.

Because of his son's rebellion he only brought things home for Katy. What disturbed Kyle Sr. the most was the fact that his negligent behavior had not bothered his son in the least.

In the summer of 1992 Kyle Sr. returned home early from work to find Kyle in bed naked with another boy from his school. He went ballistic. He barely gave the other boy an opportunity to put his clothes on before he chased him out of the house. It was then that he decided that if Kyle wasn't going to listen to reason he would beat reason into him. He entered Kyle's bedroom and closed the door behind him. He undid his belt and savagely beat his son. Returning from the grocery store with Katy, Katherine could hear her son's screams for help as she opened the front door of the house. In a panic she dropped her grocery bag and ran up the staircase to his aid. She was mortified when she opened his bedroom door and saw her husband standing over Kyle's naked body. Kyle had been beaten with the buckle of the belt and his skin had been lacerated in several places.

"What are you doing!" Katy shrieked as she ran into the room past Katherine and flung herself between her father and brother. "Leave him alone!" she continued.

Kyle Sr. shook himself as if being awakened from a trance. He looked at Katy whose eyes were filled with anger and tears, and he dropped his belt. Katherine, who was standing in the doorway of her son's room, turned and ran back down the stairs.

"Get out of here and leave him alone!" Katy screamed again.

Kyle Sr. looked at the quivering body of his son and at the wounds that he'd inflicted and left the room. Katy covered her brother and helped him up. Welts formed over the white skin of his arms, chest, back, and legs. Katy did her best to clean his wounds. Kyle winced and whimpered as she applied antiseptic to his cuts.

Not wanting to take him to the hospital, Kyle Sr. called a doctor friend of his to look after his son. The doctor owed Kyle Sr. a favor and could be counted on to be discreet.

Nothing and no one was the same in the Jennings household after that night, especially Kyle. His immediate circle of friends changed, his personality changed, and his habits changed. He started skipping classes. He quit the tennis team at his high school, and became even more withdrawn. Even his relationship with Katy deteriorated. Secrecy and suspicion shrouded the special bond and closeness they shared. Driving home from school one afternoon Katy spotted him with a group of his "new friends", hanging out in the park. From her vantagepoint she could see that they were smoking. Knowing the reputation of a couple of the guys she recognized from school she knew that they were not smoking cigarettes.

When Katy confronted Kyle about what she'd seen they argued. "I swear I will never speak to you again if you tell mom and dad," Kyle said bitterly.

Much to her regret, Katy never said a word. Kyle graduated from smoking marijuana to snorting cocaine and shooting up. He was determined to pull as far away from his white bread, upper middle class, and pompous close-minded father as he possibly could.

By the fall of 1993 Kyle was so strung out he was uncontrollable. *"Can you love me better dead than you did while I was alive?"* Those were the cryptic words that were scrawled in lipstick on the mirror in Kyle's bathroom. Katherine found him the morning of his 16th birthday lying face down on his bathroom floor. He had choked on his own vomit after swallowing a bottle of barbiturates he found in her medicine cabinet.

After Kyle's death there was plenty of guilt, blame, and anger to go around. Kyle Sr. did not make senior partner at Whitlow and Bates. Their reason was that they had decided not to bring on any new partners at the time but he knew that it had more to do with his son's suicide than they let on. He stayed on as an associate at the firm but the scandal hung heavy over his head. Unwilling to accept his role in Kyle's suicide, he started to blame and resent Katy for keeping her brother's drug abuse a secret. But they had all known that something was wrong. Still, he pushed her away.

Love or anything remotely resembling familial affection had been sorely lacking in the Jennings household long before Kyle's suicide. Katy was also a victim. In an effort to find what she wasn't getting at home, Katy found solace in the arms of her boyfriend Scott. She wanted to believe that someone loved her even if it was a lie. Katy never felt particularly attractive. In spite of her mother's wishes, she preferred blue jeans to dresses, and makeup was totally out of the question. However, nature called on her despite the lack luster way she liked to dress. She blossomed from adolescent tomboy to budding young woman seemingly overnight. She and Scott hadn't dated for very long when he began to pressure her for sex. His argument was that of a typical teen-angst ridden boy, if she truly loved him she would give herself to him. Katy never wanted to believe that her virginity was the price she had to pay for her admission of love. However, with things the way they were at home, she couldn't take the chance that Scott would push her away too. Frustration, guilt, a need for attention those were all the things that finally lead Katy to have sex with Scott. She knew that it really wasn't the kind of love she wanted, but it was a whole lot more than she had been getting at home. Gonorrhea was Scott's way of saying "thank you."

Katy knew that if her parents ever found out it would destroy whatever bond the family had left. Her situation was nothing to make light of. She discreetly inquired as to the most effective and expedient way to "take care" of her problem and sought out the free clinic. Antibiotics eventually took care of her medical condition but the humiliation and degradation of her first sexual experience would be with her forever.

There she sat in the darkness of her bedroom peering out the window over the rain-drenched streets. Her shoulder length sandy blonde hair pulled back and tied with a red ribbon. Kyle had given her the ribbon as a gift on her 9th birthday. It wasn't much, but it was the most precious gift she had besides her virginity and now *that* was gone. She pulled the ribbon from her hair and let her hair fall freely framing her face. She wrapped the ribbon around her finger as if to remind herself, that there was a time, and there was a boy that loved her without reservation. Her brother…Kyle.

5

"Katy wake up!" Katherine said softly as she tried to shake her daughter awake. "Katy," she said again. "It's time to get up. You've got a plane to catch."

With everything that had gone wrong over the past year the only thing that Katy had to look forward to was going away to college. She had been accepted to Northwestern University, her father's alma mater, shortly after Kyle's death. Katy couldn't wait to get on that plane and get as far away from Youngstown as possible.

The last breakfast she had with her mother and father was no different than the others had been since Kyle's suicide. The absence of her twin brother was still very much an issue in the house. Kyle Sr. took on more work at his firm just to keep away from home. Katherine, who had known that her husband had been having an affair for some time, was looking more haggard by the day. Katy sat looking at them both as if she were looking at strangers. "Who are these people?" she thought as she picked at her breakfast.

"Come along Katy and I'll drive you to the airport on my way to work." Kyle announced as he drank the last of his coffee.

Katy pushed her plate away, got up from the table, and went into the living room to retrieve her luggage. Katherine sat at the table and stared coldly at her husband as he pulled on his suit jacket and began to help Katy. After the car was loaded with her things, Katy went back into the kitchen to say goodbye to her mother.

"Are you sure you don't want to come to the airport with us?" she said giving Katherine an uncharacteristic embrace.

"I'm sure," Katherine responded. "You know that I'll only get emotional and you know how your father hates it when I get emotional."

Katherine pulled away from Katy and took her face in her hands. She gently pushed the hair away from Katy's eyes with her fingers. "You were always the strong one," she said as tears began to well up in her eyes. "Never forget that I tried to love you the best way I knew how," Katherine continued as she tightly embraced Katy again.

"I'll be home for Thanksgiving mom, I promise," Katy said reassuringly.

The blaring car horn interrupted the first tender moment Katy had had with her mother in what seemed a lifetime.

"You had better get going," Katherine said. "You don't want to keep your father waiting."

With that Katy backed toward the door holding onto her mother's hand as she too had started to tear up. Katherine offered her a wry smile and a knowing nod as she let go of her hand. As Katy exited through the kitchen door and jumped into the car, Katherine pressed her hand to the glass and waved goodbye. As the Mercedes motored up the driveway Katherine let go of the pain that she had held in her heart. She cried tears of release for the loss of her children, the loss of her husband, and the loss of herself.

* * * * * * * * *

"It's not your fault," Kyle Sr. said as he pulled up into the airport terminal. He put the car in park but left it running with the air-conditioner on. It was the first time he had spoken since pulling away from the house. Katy was caught totally off guard. She didn't know quite what to make of his statement. At first she thought that he might have been referring to Kyle Jr.'s suicide but before she had time to respond Kyle continued. "Your mother didn't want me to tell you, but I think you have a right to know... We're getting a divorce," he said quietly almost ashamed, but he never made eye contact. "Divorce?" Katy countered. "Divorce!" she repeated. Of all the inopportune times to shatter the last vestiges of their family existence he would have to choose the day she was going away to college. "Why are you telling me this now!" Katy said trying not to sound emotional.

Kyle took a deep breath and said calmly, "I think you know that your mother and I have had our share of problems. It hasn't been easy over the last few years. Your brother's suicide and my problems at work..."

"What problems?" Katy questioned. "Oh you mean your not making partner!" she continued sarcastically. "Or the fact that you're *making it* with one of the partners!"

Shock and surprise swept across Kyle's face as he looked at Katy for the first time.

"Don't look so surprised dad," Katy said turning away from him and glaring out the window. "I heard you and mom arguing about your affair months ago! The only thing that bothers me is why you took so long, and why you chose now to tell me about it?"

Kyle stared at his daughter for several minutes before he spoke again. "This thing with me and your mother...its no big deal. People get divorced all the time. I will still support your mother financially that won't change. And I will support you too. You are my little girl. You will always be able to count on me for what ever you need. I'll always be there for you."

"Really!" Katy said sharply. "Just like you were there for your son!" Peering at him through her sunglasses Katy was glad that her father was unable to see the tears that welled up in her eyes as she spoke. Despite her promise to come home for Thanksgiving she felt that once she boarded the plane for Evanston she would never have to see her family again. But then again she thought as she threw her head back to keep the tears from falling, she didn't really have any family left.

"Do you need any more money?" Kyle said hurriedly as he reached into the inside pocket of his suit jacket. "Here. Take this. It's $1500 and the phone number of where I'll be if you need anything more, anything at all."

Katy looked into her father's eyes and saw the guilt and the shame that had been eating at him. Those same blue eyes that she used to watch light up every time he talked about an exciting court case. She noticed, as if for the first time, the amount of gray hair he'd accumulated. This once energetic vigorously handsome figure of a man now looked old and tired. The effects of Kyle's drug abuse and subsequent suicide changed him. And now with this new revelation she could no longer stand the sight of him at all. She wanted to make her father suffer more by making some grand gesture like throwing the money in his face. She was hurt... she wasn't stupid. She knew that she could use the money. She took the envelope from his hands and stuffed it into her purse. "I've got to check in!" she announced as she opened the car door. The air-conditioner had been running the entire time but the air inside the car felt stifling compared to the relief she felt once on the outside. It was 7 o'clock in the morning on one of the hottest days in August they had seen. The sun seemed already at its highest peak. Even with the 90-degree temperature the air outside seemed easier to breathe than the air-conditioned air inside the car.

After her luggage was checked in Kyle reached out to Katy for a good-bye hug. Katy pulled away and quietly said without looking at him, "Good-bye dad," as she turned away and disappeared through the sliding glass doors and headed into the terminal.

Katy stared out the window of Delta flight 247 as it pierced through the clouds. Despite herself the tears that she'd fought to hold at bay started to flow. All of her anger, all of her hurt, all of her frustration washed over her like an uncontrollable torrent. The world that she had known was gone. All she had left to hold onto was uncertainty. She was afraid and she felt totally alone. A flight attendant came by and asked if Katy was all right, or if she was ill and needed a doctor. Unable to speak, Katy covered her face with one hand and pushed the flight attendant away with the other. As the plane ascended further into the sky Katy started to realize that even though the future was a scary place, she was turning the page on a new chapter in her life. Northwestern University was going to open up new doors and opportunities for her. A new place, a new life, a new Katy.

6

It was a week packed full of excitement. Incoming freshmen were frantically moving through registration, class sign-up, dorm assignments, and one endless orientation after another. Katy ended up on the fourth floor of Allison Hall. When she got to her room she discovered that her roommate had already beaten her to the best spot in the room by the window. Katy was a little peeved but tried not to show it.

"Hi, I'm Denise," the young girl said extending a friendly hand. "Denise McKenzie...Welcome to Allison Hall...I guess we'll be roommies this semester."

"Katy Jennings," Katy replied returning the gesture.

Katy flung her suitcases onto the empty bed by the door and slumped down beside them.

"Long day, huh?" Denise inquired. Katy nodded in response and flashed a half-hearted smile. "I saved you some closet space," Denise said as she continued to hang her favorite poster of Kenny G. on the wall. "Is that all you have?" Denise questioned turning to notice that Katy only had three pieces of luggage.

"No," Katy responded. "The rest of my things are being shipped."

"Oh my," Denise teased as she made gestures of royalty. "All right for the rest of your things being shipped. You go girl!"

Katy was a little taken aback by Denise's familiarity. She was even more surprised to note that Denise was black. Not that she minded, it was just that she had not known what to expect. Katy just sat there on the edge of her bed and watched Denise move about the room hanging posters of various jazz musicians and arraying the bureau with framed pictures of loved ones.

Denise laughed to herself as she misinterpreted the expression on Katy's face.

Denise McKenzie was the youngest of five children. Born and reared in Indianapolis, Indiana. She graduated from Lawrence Central High School with a GPA of 3.9. She was as beautiful as she was intelligent, and she was very talkative. From the time she was born she was taught to overlook racism as ignorance no matter how subtle. She wrongly assumed that Katy was both. Her father Dr. Philip McKenzie, taught her, as well as her other sisters and brothers, that the only way to make it in the world is to show people how good you are not how bad they think you are. He taught them never to settle for second best.

"Unless you've decided to change rooms or something you may as well make yourself at home." Denise chattered on without missing a beat. "I've left you plenty of wall space if you've got pictures or something that you want to put up. Uhm...By the way you're not a devil worshipper or anything are you?"

"Devil worshipper?" Katy inquired.

"You know like killing cats or drinking blood or anything like that," Denise pressed.

"What's your blood type?" Katy asked wryly.

"B positive," Denise warily responded.

"That figures! Sorry you're not my type at all!" Katy sarcastically remarked.

It took about a half a minute for Denise to realize that Katy was pulling her leg. Her mouth dropped opened as it dawned on her that Katy was joking.

"You know you're all right Katy Jennings," Denise laughed. "I think we're going to get along just fine."

Katy laughed too. It was the first time in a long time that the wry sense of humor that Kyle Jr. used to love about her surfaced from behind the dark cloud of her pain.

Katy went to the closet to hang up some of her clothes and began to admire the chic and sophisticated clothes that Denise had. Katy's clothes were all right, but compared to Denise she felt her things were strictly bargain basement.

Katy finished unpacking and putting her things away and pulled a picture from her bag and gingerly positioned it on the nightstand next to her bed.

"Is that your family?" Denise inquired.

"Yeah this is my mom and dad and me and my twin brother Kyle." Katy said proudly.

"He's cute," Denise gushed. "What's he doing now? Is he in college? Is he married? Is he gay?"

"He's dead," Katy responded flatly.

Not knowing quite what to say Denise clumsily stumbled through an apology. The room fell silent but the tension was soon broken by a squeal from the other side of the door. "Denise, open the door it's me Ashley!"

Happy for the distraction, Denise bounded off her bed without a second thought and flung the door open. Ashley pushed her way in giggling and staggering not waiting for an invitation.

"Girl what is wrong with you?" Denise asked trying to hold back an all out laugh. "Have you been drinking?"

"No!" Ashley replied as she sprawled across Denise's bed. "I'm just bored. I wanna shop! I wanna meet some men! I wanna party!"

Katy sat quietly on her bed observing Ashley.

"Oh sorry," Ashley continued as she acknowledged Katy. "You must be *'the roommate',*" she said stiffly as she sat up on the bed and ran her fingers through her short auburn locks. "I'm Ashley... *'the next door neighbor'.*"

"Katy Jennings," she responded extending her hand.

"That's so cute," Ashley teased looking at Katy's hand. "You must have learned that from Denise."

Katy pulled back her hand and wiped it on the leg of her jeans as if it had been spit on.

Ashley Gibson was from Champaign, Illinois and she was a self-absorbed snob. She wanted what she wanted when she wanted it, and if you were in her way she plowed right through you. Like Denise, Ashley was very trendy. She kept up with the latest fashions and the latest hairstyles. Katy was really starting to feel like a fish out of water. Ashley had a way of looking at you through her green eyes that made you feel more like the hired help than one of her peers. Katy found it strange that someone like Denise could be a friend with someone like Ashley. Denise and Ashley actually met during pre-registration earlier that summer and they seemed to hit it off right away. Katy was unable to attend the orientation because she had a bout with the flu.

However, Ashley had a vulnerable and needy side that she learned to keep hidden. Like Katy, Ashley's home life wasn't picture perfect either, and that would soon prove to be the bridge to a relationship of familiarity for them both.

"I've got a great idea!" Denise exclaimed. "Why don't we drive down to Chicago, have dinner, and then we can go check out my boyfriend's band. They're playing tonight at this club on Halstead."

"That *is* a great idea!" Ashley squealed with excitement. "I've got this hot new outfit that I've just been dying to wear!"

"What about you Katy?" Denise inquired.

Katy shrugged her shoulders and said, "You guys go ahead. I'm just gonna take a walk around campus and read or something."

"Well it's settled then," Ashley said turning away from Katy. "It'll just be me and Denise."

"No, no, no," Denise interrupted. "Katy I really think you should come with us. You look like you could use some fun."

"I'll be fine by myself," Katy said looking at the picture of her family on the nightstand.

Denise followed Katy's eyes and remembered what she said about her brother before Ashley came into the room. "You're going!" Denise demanded putting her hands on her hips. Ashley and Katy both turned to her with surprised looks on their faces. "You're going and that's final!"

After a few more minutes of chatter about what they were going to wear, Ashley went to her room to get dressed. After she had gone Denise walked over to the closet and started rummaging through it. "I'm not going to be trapped all semester with a stick in the mud!" Denise said as she continued to go through the closet trying not to notice Katy's clothes. "You're going with us and you're going to have fun or else!" Just as she finished her statement, Denise emerged from the closet with one of her dresses. She tossed the dress over to Katy, "I think that one should fit...Try it on!" she insisted. Katy looked at the dress and ran her hands over the fabric. Her face lit up as she turned to Denise and said "thank you."

Katy showered and changed from her tight jeans and tennis shoes into the floral print silk spaghetti strapped dress. Looking at herself in the mirror Katy was moved to tears as she admired the way the cut of the dress accentuated the curve of her body. Denise even helped her with her make-up and hair. "With the right application of makeup any girl can look like a woman," Denise rationalized. "What would mom think of me now," Katy wondered as she preened in front of the mirror in her room. Ashley was stunned when she returned and saw the transformation Katy had undergone. "All right girl you get points for that!" Ashley snapped as she sashayed into the room.

On the ride to Chicago the ice between Ashley and Katy started to melt as they discovered that they had more in common than either of them realized. Ashley actually opened up and shared that she was an only child and that her mother and father divorced when she was 12 years old. She joked about how her mother remarried and divorced again practically before the ink was dry on the first divorce decree. "My step father had more money than my father did anyway," Ashley quipped. "He was always buying me stuff. Sometimes he treated me better than he treated my...." Ashley caught herself before she finished her statement realizing that she was divulging just a little too much information. Denise glanced back at Katy in the rear view mirror. Katy was looking at Ashley who had turned to stare out the passenger window. Despite the music on the radio, a caustic silence came over the three girls. Katy looked as if she knew the conclusion of what Ashley was about to say but she dared not press her to finish.

The Gemini was one of the newest, trendiest, and the hottest clubs in Chicago. There was definitely the 'who's who' element among the throng of patrons vying to get in. It took nearly an hour but Katy, Ashley, and Denise finally managed to get to the front of the line. Although she was not yet 21 Denise had ID that proved otherwise, as did Ashley. When it came to Katy the bouncer was a little harder to convince. Ashley had given her an ID that she had taken a year prior when she was a blonde but her eye's told a different story. The bouncer shined his flashlight on the ID and then into Katy's face. "Contacts!" Ashley yelled over the pulse of the music. "Haven't you ever seen a girl wear contacts?" The bouncer was still not convinced. Just as he was about ready to eject the trio from the line a tall, good looking, well dressed black man stepped up to the bouncer shook a hundred-dollar bill into his hand, flashed a smile and winked. "They're with me Otis," he said as he put his hand in the small of Katy's back. The bouncer smiled back at the man and motioned his head toward the door to signal that it was all right for the girls to enter.

Once inside the club the mysterious stranger commandeered a table for the ladies and he took it upon himself to join them. "Excuse me but we don't know you!" Ashley sneered. "Sure you do," said the man with a bit of a drawl. "I just paid an extra $100 for you ladies to come in here and enjoy the ambiance. I'd say that ought to make us at least social to one another," he continued flashing a big wide grin. "What do you think beautiful?" he said winking at Katy. "He did get us in here Ashley," Katy said sheepishly. "If it wasn't for him we'd be on our way back to Evanston."

Ashley huffed and rolled her eyes and looked away. Denise looked at Katy and then she looked at the stranger. When he returned her stare a chill ran down her spine and she looked away.

"Can I get anybody anything to drink?" said the female server as she approached their table.

"I'll have coffee," said the stranger. "And you can get these ladies anything they want… on me."

"I'll have a gin and tonic!" Ashley piped up cutting her eyes toward the stranger. "Make it a double!"

"Can you tell me where I can find Randy Elliot the saxophone player for the band tonight?" Denise asked.

"The band is back in the dressing room getting ready for their next set," the server responded.

"Do you think you could tell Randy that Denise is here?" Denise requested.

"Yeah I can do that," replied the server. "In the mean time can I get you something from the bar?"

"I'll just have a ginger ale," Denise said. "I'll have a ginger ale too" Katy chimed in.

"Ginger ale?" Ashley grimaced. "I can see that you two aren't going to be any fun at all!"

* * * * * * * * * *

Denise sat gawking at Randy like the love struck teenager she was as the band began their second set. Ashley moved to the bar and had become the center of attention for three male admirers. Katy sat quietly slowly nursing her ginger ale as she listened to the band and watched the sights around her with the wide-eyed amazement of a child.

"You don't talk much do you?" inquired the stranger trying to get Katy's attention. "You've never been in a place like this before have you?" he continued. Katy looked at him embarrassed that her actions had given her away. "How old are you really?" he pressed. Katy's response was interrupted as the sound of uproarious laughter drew their attention to the bar. "Your friend seems to be having a pretty good time doesn't she?"

"Yes she does," Katy said as she looked back to the attentive stranger. Despite the smell of cigarette smoke in the room she was captivated by the allure of his cologne. She took a deep breath as she noted the amount of sugar he poured into his coffee. "You think you might like a little coffee to go with all that sugar?" Katy teased. The man looked at her and laughed a deep resonant laugh as he rubbed his hand over his clean-shaven head. "You know we've been sitting here for almost an hour and you still haven't told us who you are," she continued.

"Well I'll tell you a secret," he said in a low seductive whisper as he moved closer to Katy. "My real name is Albert..." he began as he entwined his fingers in the strap of her dress, "...but everybody calls me... Sugar Man."

The pun was not lost on Katy as she covered her mouth to quiet her laughter.

* * * * * * * * *

Katy sat behind the wheel of Denise's car as the trio made their way back to the university. Ashley was laid across the back seat sleeping off the alcohol that would soon enough turn into a *queen*-sized headache. Denise was on the passenger side reading a letter that Randy had written her. She was all smiles as she read and reminisced about the few stolen moments they had together after the club closed for the night. Katy too was all smiles as she reflected on the handsome stranger that had so overwhelmed her. She could still smell his cologne. She could still feel the touch of his fingers on her shoulder. She touched her hand to the cheek that he had gently kissed as he pressed his phone number into her hand. She felt tingly all over as she whispered his name and smiled, "Sugar Man."

7

Despite the late hour that they returned from Chicago, Katy got up early the next morning to call Sugar Man as she promised. "I'm glad you called," he whispered. His voice was gravelly but it sounded very sensual to Katy. Speaking softly into the phone so not to wake Denise, Katy apologized for calling so early explaining that he asked her to call as soon as she woke up. He had no way of knowing that she was an early riser. Sugar Man cleared his throat and encouraged her to talk to him.

Sugar Man had an appeal that was totally disarming. He was as charming as he was handsome. Men found it hard to compete with him and women found it hard to resist him. He possessed an arrogance that was almost admirable. And he was a man of mystery. No one knew exactly where he came from or what he was after half the time, and he liked it like that.

When he talked Katy marveled at the fact that his words and the sound of his voice were as hypnotic as the smell of his cologne had been. They talked for a few minutes and before she knew it she had agreed to have lunch with him. Sugar Man offered to drive to Evanston to pick her up, Katy did not refuse. She wouldn't have even if she wanted to. For some unexplained reason she felt that she would be able to tell him anything no matter how obscure, and he would listen to her. Her brother Kyle had been the only one in her life that she had been able to open up to in such a manner.

With butterflies in her stomach Katy got off the phone and went to the closet to try and find something to wear for her lunch date. As she rummaged through the clothes in her closet she was annoyed that none of her clothes would be suitable enough to be seen with the caliber of man that Sugar Man obviously was.

"What are you doing?" Denise questioned as she rolled over and looked at the pile of clothes that Katy had thrown on the floor.

"I'm trying to find something to wear!" Katy responded.

"Wear? Where are you going? What time is it?" countered Denise.

"I don't have any descent clothes!" Katy shrieked angrily as she threw herself hopelessly onto her bed. How she had wished she had listened to her mother all those times she had tried to get her to dress more fashionably and buy nicer, more feminine attire.

Denise raised up, looked at the clock on her night table and with an exasperated sigh fell back into her pillows. "Girl...it's Saturday morning and it's too early. If you don't stop making all that noise and go back to sleep I will hurt you!"

Undaunted Katy opened the drawer to her nightstand and pulled out the envelope with the $1500 in it that she had hidden in a book. "Shopping!" she exclaimed. Realizing that she wouldn't have enough time to go shopping before it was time for her date she got up from the bed and went back to the closet. This time she went through Denise's things.

"Denise are you asleep?" Katy whispered holding up one of Denise's outfits. "Denise...Denise can I wear this?"

Denise did not respond. Katy had not asked the question in such a way to solicit a response let alone to allow Denise to hear her. Katy had justified that because Denise had been so accommodating the night before that she wouldn't mind if she wore something else of hers. There was no way she was going to let this man think that she had no style at all.

Sugar Man picked Katy up in the pre-designated meeting place. He pulled his fire red convertible Mercedes up to the curb where she was waiting, jumped out, and opened her door for her. Katy felt a tinge of nervousness as he brushed his lips against her cheek and said in his sensual low drawl "Hello beautiful." Never in her life had she been treated in such a way and she loved every minute of it.

As they drove up the street the warm August breeze gave Katy a rush of excitement. The silk material of her blouse flapped softly across her bare skin. She threw her head back and let the wind blow through her hair. Katy felt a guilty pleasure that she had sneaked away from the campus with only a note to Denise that she would be back later. Adventure was waiting for her she mused, adventure and a man of mystery.

"I have to make a stop!" Sugar Man said as he rounded Michigan Avenue. He pulled his Mercedes up to the intercom connected to a garage attached to a high-rise building off Lakeshore Drive.

"It's me!" he announced to the man on the other end of the intercom. The system buzzed and the gates to the garage opened allowing Sugar Man to pull his car in. He parked the car and went around to the passenger side to open the door for Katy. They took the garage elevator up to the 22nd floor. Katy thought she was dreaming as she marveled at the opulence of the building when they stepped off the elevator. But that was nothing in comparison to what her eyes witnessed once the door to the apartment opened.

They were greeted at the door by a tall muscular black man with curly black hair and deep set hazel eyes. After the brief introductions he ushered them in and offered them something to drink. Katy accepted, Sugar Man declined. He addressed the man very sternly and told him that they needed to take care of business. The man smiled at Sugar Man and then to Katy. "All right" he said. "Business it is." The man directed Sugar Man into another room and turned to take Katy into the kitchen. When he opened the door to the kitchen Katy saw another man seated at the table. Much younger than the one who had greeted them. He sat shirtless and totally oblivious to the fact that Katy and the other man were in the room. He had headphones on and his head was bobbing up and down to the pulse of the music that could be heard despite the fact that he had on headphones. His attention was drawn to the comic book that he was reading as he continued to shovel cereal into his mouth.

"K.C.!" the man shouted trying to get his attention. "K.C.!" he said again as he stepped over to him and pulled off his headphones.

K.C. jumped startled that someone was in the room. He looked up directly into Katy's face. He was beautiful she thought. His dark masculine features on his evenly copper toned skin. At 19 years old K.C. (Keith) had grown from an awkward teen to a strikingly handsome young man. The peach fuzz that used to reside above his upper lip had grown into a distinguishable mustache. The only evidence of the beating that he suffered upon his arrival to Chicago was a scar that cut through his left brow, but even that gave him more of a sensual quality.

"I'm sorry," he blurted out. "I didn't hear anybody come in."

"K.C. this is Katy," said the man. "Entertain her for a few minutes, I got some business with Sugar in the other room."

K.C. nodded and the man left the room. K.C. motioned for Katy to sit down and offered her something to drink. "So you're Sugar's new girl," K.C. said as he poured orange juice into a glass for Katy.

"New girl?" Katy mused as she took a sip from the glass. "This is such a great place! Is Drake your dad?" Katy questioned.

"You could say that," K.C. responded.

Katy and K.C.'s polite conversation was interrupted as a longhaired Persian cat jumped up on the table.

"Pickles get down!" K.C. shouted as he tried to brush her away.

"No it's okay," Katy said comfortingly picking the cat up and nuzzling her with her chin. "She's beautiful! Why do you call her Pickles?"

"Because she's weird! She likes to eat pickles," K.C. responded. "Besides Drake named her…not me."

As Katy continued to caress the cat's fur, Sugar Man entered the kitchen with Drake in tow. Sugar Man acknowledged K.C. and informed Katy that it was time to go. Katy put Pickles down on the floor as the cat continued to nudge up against her leg.

"I think she likes you," Drake said smiling as he bent over and picked the cat up. Sugar Man took Katy by the hand and led her from the kitchen. "It was nice meeting you K.C." Katy said as she turned and left the kitchen. Drake followed them and showed them to the door.

* * * * * * * * *

Sugar Man slammed on the brakes of his Mercedes as he exited the parking garage. He laid on the car horn as he saw an old man standing in front of the car holding up a sign that read 'REPENT FOR THE KINGDOM OF HEAVEN IS AT HAND.' Through her sunglasses Katy could sense the piercing gaze of the old man. She rubbed her throat as she felt it go dry at the sensation that he generated in her.

"Get out of the way old man!" Sugar Man yelled as he continued to blast the horn.

The old man didn't move. He stood there at the opening of the garage in his dirty tattered clothing and stared directly at Katy. She looked away from him and to Sugar Man as if imploring him to do something. When she looked back the old man was gone. The tires of the Mercedes screeched as Sugar Man floored the accelerator and sped away from the building.

* * * * * * * * *

"So you like cats huh?" It was the second time Sugar Man had asked Katy a question since they sat down in the restaurant, he could sense that she was disturbed. In her mind she was back in the high-rise garage with the old man looking at her with his piercing stare. She was remembering the sign he held, 'REPENT FOR THE KINGDOM OF HEAVEN IS AT HAND', and it sent an indescribable chill through her.

"Hello!" Sugar Man said snapping his fingers in her face. "Anybody in there?"

Katy shook herself and apologized to him for zoning out. She explained to Sugar Man that she was unable to get the image of the old man out of her head. Sugar Man's expression turned sour. He sat looking at her a few seconds and then he leaned over to her and gently kissed her on the lips. "Don't think about that old man anymore baby," he said sensuously. "Think about me…. Kat."

Katy blushed and smiled as the name "Kat" danced in her head. She liked it. She liked the way it sounded. She liked the way he said it. She looked at her reflection in the window of the restaurant and stroked her hair. "Kat!" she said aloud.

"A lot of white people are afraid of a well dressed brother... I think it's the head...It intimidates 'em...Because I shave my head they think I'm militant or somethin'...But you don't seem to be afraid of me...Why not?" Sugar Man asked.

Katy shrugged her shoulders and smiled in response to Sugar Man's question. Fear wasn't what she felt. When he looked at her she felt a surge of excitement. It was the sense of excitement she often craved as she sat alone in her bedroom window in her parent's house.

* * * * * * * * * *

The afternoon she spent with Sugar Man was filled with wonderment. He took her to the top of the Sears tower. He also took her to the McCormick Center, Buckingham Fountain, and McKinley Park. They had even gone through China Town. She was euphoric as she opened the door to her dormitory room and lay back against the wall with her eyes closed reliving the events of the day.

"Well, well, well, look who's back!"

Katy opened her eyes and saw Ashley and Denise sitting on the floor eating pizza.

"Katy please don't borrow my clothes again without asking!" Denise said angrily.

"I'm sorry Denise, but I did ask!" Katy responded. "I'll have your things cleaned next week... I promise... Please just don't be mad at me... I have just had the most incredible day!"

"Please don't tell me that you actually slept with Mr. Cue ball!" Ashley shrieked.

"What makes you think I was with a man?" Katy countered.

"It was that guy from the club last night wasn't it?" inquired Denise.

Shocked, Ashley squealed "Oh my God...Did you let him..."

"...What if I did!" Katy shot back angrily.

Although she hadn't actually done anything with Sugar Man, Katy had entertained the idea. To her Sugar Man was like honey. Everything about him was like nothing she had ever known before. She felt that if she had made love with him it would not have ended like her encounter with Scott when she gave up her virginity.

"You had just better watch yourself Katy" Denise offered. "I have a bad feeling about that man. He's not being nice to you for nothing."

"I can take care of myself!" Katy said defensively. "I always have! And I always will."

Katy was beside herself with anticipation. In one afternoon Sugar Man had exposed her to all kinds of new and exciting things that she had never experienced before. He didn't treat her like a child. He treated her like a woman. He had even promised to take her to her very first Chicago Bulls basketball game. Katy didn't particularly care for sports but she felt that even that would be exciting if she was with him. However before she did anything else with Sugar Man she was going to have to do something about her clothes. She made plans to get up early the next day so that she could go shopping and redo her entire wardrobe courtesy of Kyle Sr.'s guilt.

That night visions of Sugar Man filled Katy's head. She couldn't get him out of her mind. She was aroused by the fantasy of being with him in the most intimate of ways. As she drifted into sleep another vision entered her subconscious. The vision of the old man with the piercing eyes, and the crude makeshift sign... 'REPENT FOR THE KINGDOM OF HEAVEN IS AT HAND'. Katy tossed and turned for the better part of the night as visions of the old man got stronger. Who was he? What did he want from her?

8

A lot about Keith had changed in the six years since he had come to live with Drake, not only what he called himself. He now sported two pierced ears and a tattoo displayed prominently on his left bicep. To compliment his physique and to teach him discipline, K.C. was working toward black belt status in karate largely due to Drake's encouragement.

Keith Coleman was still considered a missing person or assumed dead by the Atlanta authorities, but K.C., nobody was looking for him, least of all the police. He moved about the streets of Chicago as if he had always belonged there. Drake Sommersbee had not only befriended him; he had become his mentor. Having literally disappeared off the face of the earth at 13, K.C. had no formal education so he had no real means of support with the exception of Drake. The older he got the more curious K.C. became about everything that concerned this man. What he discovered at first repulsed and even frightened him, but he soon learned to adapt and in time became a willing if not eager participant.

By the time he was 14 years old K.C. was getting high on a regular basis. He smoked at least six or seven *joints* a day. Drake preferred cocaine to marijuana so K.C. soon developed a knack for snorting. On his 15th birthday Drake threw a surprise party for him. The surprise was that there were no women invited, at least none that were with other men. That was the day that K.C. was introduced to a very different kind of "family" unit. The day that he confirmed what he had suspected for some time, Drake Sommersbee was gay. Drake was never overtly obvious, nor was he the cliched "flaming queen." Still there had been red flags thrown up along the way. Like the way Drake would stare at K.C. as he moved about the apartment, or the fact that the only pornographic magazines he found in the house were full of men. Or the fact that the only late night, or overnight callers Drake would have were men.

K.C.'s good looks quickly made him the *"fête d'jour"* in Drake's social circles. But Drake was protective of his protégé, "lust but don't touch," was his motto. And as far as his own attraction to K.C. was concerned Drake was careful never to make any unwanted advances. He had never forced himself on K.C. or took advantage of him. And K.C. felt that Drake had been good to him. Living with him was like being on a holiday every day of the year.

K.C. knew all the guests at the party by association. He enjoyed their company even though his libido was disappointed that some of the finest women at the party were lesbians. They were a partying bunch. Despite himself he had to admit that even some of the men at the party were painfully attractive. Drake was associated with some of the most aesthetically beautiful people K.C. had ever met in his entire life.

The liquor flowed, the music pulsated and everybody was having a good time. Drake made it mandatory that everyone bring K.C. presents and K.C. loved every minute of the attention. The party carried on into the wee hours of the morning. Drake's apartment looked as if a cyclone had hit it by the time the last of his guests had gone home but he didn't care. If K.C. was happy that made Drake happy.

Late the next afternoon K.C. awoke naked in Drake's bed. He'd willingly given himself to his mentor. Surprisingly K.C. wasn't freaked out. He rationalized that it must have been something that he had subconsciously wanted to do for a long time and the alcohol and the cocaine had given him the wherewithal to do it.

Six months into this new relationship with this man he had known as his mentor he discovered how he made his money. Drake Sommersbee ran a high class male escort service and his client list contained some of the most influential men in the country. They were from all walks of life. They were doctors, and lawyers, and government officials, musicians, and actors or anyone who could afford his asking price of $1,000.

Drake had taken a friend to dinner and asked K.C. to come along. His friend was immediately taken by K.C.'s striking looks and wanted to do business. Against Drake's objections K.C. consented. It was a kick, K.C. thought, as he allowed the man to undress him. He was 15 years old and some guy was willing to pay $1,000 to have sex with him. In his whole life he never thought he would be able to make $1,000 by doing anything, let alone having sex. He never once stopped to consider the consequences. To K.C. there were no consequences.

After a while the compassion that had shown in his eyes began to fade. K.C. developed a very cynical view of life. He never really knew, or ever experienced real love. As a young boy he felt that his father loved him or at least the idea of him. "A man should have sons!" he remembered him say once. His mother's love was always conditional. If he behaved in a certain way; or did things in a certain way; or never bothered to ask for much; then she considered him to be a good son. But the minute he started wanting things that she couldn't afford to give him, as children sometimes do, he became a nuisance and a bother. She once told him in a fit of anger that the only reason she had him in the first place was because that was what his father wanted. Carla Jackson was more interested in the way men looked at her. She never thought that children should be a part of that package. And Warren, Warren never counted for much of anything. The only person in his life that came remotely close to anything that could be called *love* was Drake Sommersbee. It's a sad commentary on life when the only love you get as a child comes with a price tag on it...from everybody.

9

"Katy...This is your father...You need to come home...It's about your mother..."

Five weeks into her first semester and Katy was headed home. It seems that Katherine was no longer able to cope with the pressure that she had been under especially since Kyle Sr. was so adamant about a divorce. **KATHERINE JENNINGS WIFE OF PROMINENT YOUNGSTOWN ATTORNEY DEAD AT 44**: That's what screamed at Katy from the headlines of the VINDICATOR as she walked through the airport terminal.

Anger and rage were the only emotions sustaining Katy from the time her father called to give her the news until the time the plane touched down. She had only packed enough clothes for a couple of days and then she was going to leave Youngstown forever. As she reached out to open the door of the cab she hailed a hand grabbed her arm from behind. She turned sharply and discovered that it was her father.

"I hardly recognized you," Kyle began. He was flabbergasted by her new sense of style that had been influenced by Denise and Ashley. "Sweetheart didn't you hear me call your name inside the terminal?"

Without saying a word Katy pulled the sunglasses from her face so that her father would see just how much she hated him at that moment. Looking into the coldness of her pale blue eyes Kyle Sr. swallowed hard and let go of her arm. Katy readjusted her sunglasses turned away from her father and jumped into the cab. On her command the driver pulled away from the curb, leaving her father standing there.

* * * * * * * * *

Katy sat stalwart on the front pew of the church waiting for the service to begin. As she sat she lamented the times that she had not been particularly kind to her mother. The times when she knew that she had pushed the envelope a little too far. The times when Katherine tried to reach out to her and have real quality mother-daughter time and she dismissed her as overly emotional or sentimental. Times that she would never be able to get back. Times that she was sorry she'd lost.

Katherine Ashton Jennings hailed from Boston, Massachusetts, the only child of Paul and Vivian Ashton. Katherine was poised, articulate, and stylish, she was raised to marry the "right sort of man," have children, and be the perfect wife and mother. The world she grew up in was so much different than the world she found herself raising her children in. There was no open talk of sexuality good or bad. Certain things just were not discussed in polite society. Women were women, men were men, black was black and white was white, that's just the way it was and that's the way it should have stayed as far as Katherine was concerned.

Katherine met Kyle when he came to Boston to work for her uncle's law firm. The attraction the two shared was obvious from the beginning. Outwardly they appeared to be the perfect couple. Katherine was quite a beauty in her youth. Her long golden blonde hair accentuated by her delicate features and beguiling smile, and Kyle was the handsome idealist. Kyle didn't want children right away. He was more interested in his career and how his association with the boss' niece might propel him forward. He worked night and day to move his way through her uncle's firm only to be looked over time and again for promotion. When the opportunity came for advancement from the distinguished firm of Whitlow and Bates, Kyle jumped at the chance.

Much to Kyle's dismay, Katherine discovered that she was pregnant shortly after the couple set up house in Youngstown. To add insult to injury, Kyle discovered that the results of his wife's ultra sound revealed twins.

Practically from birth the differences between Katy and her mother were plain to see. Katy was so unlike Katherine in many ways. Not only in her attitude and the way she chose to dress, but her personality as well. Katy intentionally went out of her way to buck against Katherine's gentile nature.

"You were always the strong one." That was the last thing her mother said to her as she stood in the kitchen the morning she left for Northwestern. And as much as Katy hated to be reminded of it, she was more like her father than she cared to admit. Katy shook herself in an effort to cast off the memories and concentrate on what she must do from that day forward. She closed her eyes and tried to keep her mind from wandering. While her eyes were closed she felt a hand gently grab hers and squeeze. She opened her eyes and saw that it was her father. She pulled her hand away and moved down to the far end of the pew. Kyle could only look around in embarrassment to see which of the mourners had witnessed the scene. Katy looked at him with utter contempt. How dare he try to put on a show in front of these people. It was he who had pushed her mother to suicide just as he'd done with Kyle and she wasn't about to be a participant in his superficial facade of family solidarity.

"So this is how it is going to be?" Kyle Sr. asked as their limousine pulled away from the gravesite. "Are you planning to give me the cold shoulder for the rest of your life?"

"No!" Katy seethed. "Only for the rest of *yours*!"

"Now c'mon Katy! That's not fair!"

"So why don't you tell me what's fair dad, huh? Is it fair that mom killed herself because she had had enough heartache for one lifetime? Is it fair that you did the same thing to her that you did to Kyle? Is it fair that you get to go on with your miserable life with your little office slut while my brother and my mother are dead...because of you? It was all about you and what you wanted and what you needed! Did you ever once stop to consider what she wanted or what she needed? Did you ever care? She *needed* you! Kyle *needed* you! I *needed* you!"

Katy was determined not to crack. She had not shed one tear since she was told that her mother was dead and she wasn't about to break down in front of her father. She just stared at him with the intensity of a steamroller and he just stared back with his mouth agape at the stinging truth of her tirade.

Kyle knew that any more words from him at that point would prove futile. He allowed Katy the solitude in the family home that she had requested even though he knew that once she returned to Northwestern he might not ever see her again.

* * * * * * * * *

The flight back to Evanston seemed longer than the first time she had gone this route. Unlike the first time Katy was much less emotional. She was almost catatonic as she stared straight ahead. There were no words. There were no tears. There was no feeling.

When she got back to her room at Allison Hall, Katy discovered that Denise had gone for the weekend. "Great!" Katy thought she didn't feel like seeing anybody anyway. She threw her bag on the floor and stretched out across her bed. She had almost drifted off to sleep when Ashley came knocking.

"Katy! Katy it's me Ashley! Open the door!"

"Go away!" Katy shouted.

"I'm not going away until you open the door!" Ashley retorted through slurred speech.

Katy roused herself up from the bed and opened the door. It was obvious to her that Ashley had been drinking.

"Ashley I just got back and I really don't feel up to talking to anybody right now so if you don't mind..."

In her characteristic way of not waiting for an invitation Ashley pushed her way into the room with a bottle of gin in one hand and a half full glass in the other. She sat down on Denise's bed and scanned the room as if looking for something.

"Denise and her boyfriend drove up to India-no-place for the weekend," Ashley whined as she started to cry. "I don't want to be alone right now...I really need someone to talk to."

Katy sighed heavily, closed the door and sat down on her bed.

"I wish my mother was dead!" Ashley blurted out. Katy was struck by the insensitivity of Ashley's statement. "My mother found out about me and my stepfather this weekend. She threw me out of the house. Can you imagine that? She's keeping him and she threw me out! What kind of a mother does that to her own daughter, huh? She said taking another swig from the glass. "Here you want some of this?" she continued, offering the bottle of gin to Katy. Katy shook her head and waved the bottle away. "What? You to good to drink with me? Your family ain't so perfect either you know missy!"

Katy thought about what Ashley said. She thought about the last 48 hours. She thought about her mother and Kyle. She thought that she had been thinking too much. She grabbed a glass from the desk at the foot of her bed and hesitantly poured a small amount of gin into the glass.

"Atta girl!" Ashley encouraged.

Katy slowly put the glass to her lips and let the pungent odor of the liquor waft up to her nose. She held her breath and threw back her head and in one gulp consumed the first taste of alcohol she had ever had. Katy choked and coughed as the gin burned a path down her throat to her stomach. After a few seconds the sensation to gag had passed and in its wake left Katy with a desire for more. The more gin they consumed the more she and Ashley commiserated. The more they commiserated the more gin they consumed.

* * * * * * * * *

The telephone rang and broke into the silence of the room. Ashley was sprawled out on the floor and Katy lay half off the bed. She jumped with a start as if a fire alarm had gone off after she had detected the sixth or seventh ring. She clumsily pulled the phone toward her and picked up the receiver. "Kat... are you there?" came a low familiar drawl from the other end. "Kat? It's me Sugar... I just called to check on you to make sure that you were all right and that you had made it back from Ohio in one piece. Katy grabbed her head with her free hand and pulled herself up on the bed.

"I missed you," she whispered.

"I missed you too baby... I wanna see you."

"I wanna see you too."

"Hey if it's too soon I'll understand. I don't want you to feel rushed."

"No... I don't feel rushed. I really wanna see you...Today."

When she hung up the phone she looked at the clock on her nightstand. The display read three o'clock. She had slept through the night and into the better part of Sunday afternoon. She then noticed the picture of her family out of the frame and in pieces on the floor. She knelt down and picked the pieces up and arranged them back together on her nightstand. As she did she remembered that at some point during the night she had ripped the picture up in a fit of anger. Her eyes started to cloud as she thought back on the old Mother Goose nursery rhyme. *Humpty Dumpty sat on the wall. Humpty Dumpty had a great fall. All the kings' horses and all the kings' men couldn't put Humpty together again.* "I gotta get up!" she said aloud as she crumpled the loose pieces of the picture in her hands and threw them in the trash.

10

It was November; a month after her mother's funeral and the effects of the loss had finally started to show. Katy's grades were slipping and she had started skipping classes all together.

"What'll ya' have?" said the bartender trying to be heard over all the noise in the club.

"Ginger ale!" Katy yelled. "On second thought make that gin without the ginger and without the ale!"

"Looks like somebody is out to party!" a male voice said from behind her.

Katy whipped around and there standing behind her was K.C.

"Hi!" Katy shrieked as she bounced up and down on the barstool to the beat of the music.

"Are you here alone?" K.C. asked.

"No! Sugar is around here somewhere!" she said as she scanned the crowd trying to locate him.

"What about you?" Katy responded. "Are you here alone?"

"No…I'm on a *date*!" K.C. grimaced.

"Oh…Where's Drake?" Katy continued as she reached for the drink the bartender set before her. "Don't worry Sugar told me all about you and Drake…I'm not freaked out or anything."

"He's not feeling too good so he stayed in tonight." K.C. offered.

The bartender took K.C.'s order and then filled it while he stood and talked with Katy. As they talked Katy spotted Sugar Man through the crowd pressed in the corner with another woman and a twinge of jealousy came over her.

"Do you know who that is over there with Sugar Man?" she asked K.C. trying not to sound suspicious.

"Her name's Cookie," K.C. responded as he retrieved his drinks from the bar. "Hey you wanna come over to my table until Sugar Man gets back?"

Katy peered over K.C.'s shoulder to the man sitting at the table trying to be inconspicuous.

"Hey... Isn't that..." Katy inquired.

"...Yeah but don't tell anybody or my reputation will be ruined!" K.C. laughed as he turned to go back to his table.

A few minutes later Sugar Man returned to Katy at the bar. "I'm sorry baby," he said as he kissed Katy on the neck. "Business... you understand." He sat on the stool next to Katy and ordered a coffee with lots of sugar. "When did you start drinking?" he questioned as he noticed her glass.

"Apparently we have a lot to learn about each other!" Katy shot back.

"What do you mean by that?" he responded.

"Exactly what kind of business are you in?" Katy asked looking directly into his eyes.

Sugar Man's eyes narrowed returning her direct gaze as he spoke. "You asked me that before Kat, and when I started to tell you, you told me you didn't want to know. Now are you so sure you're really ready for an answer to that question?"

Katy nodded hesitantly as Sugar Man took a drink of his coffee. "I'm a pharmacist," he whispered into her ear.

The way in which he said "pharmacist" and the tone that he used gave Katy pause. She looked into his eyes and instinctively knew that there was something more. She thought about her brother Kyle and the type of people that he associated with after she discovered his drug abuse. His supplier was not slick, sophisticated, or well dressed, but this was not Youngstown, Ohio, this was Chicago.

"Do you deal drugs?" Katy asked flatly.

"I prefer to give it a more clinical spin," he said in a low hushed voice.

Katy sat for a few minutes contemplating what he said and suddenly she grabbed her purse, jumped off the barstool, and bolted for the door. Sugar Man rushed after her.

"Whoa wait a minute!" he said grabbing her arm. "You wanted to know. Now you know and this is how you're gonna act?"

"Both my brother and my mother died of a drug overdose!" Katy shouted. "You know how I feel about drugs!"

The disturbance caused the bar patrons closest to the couple to turn and stare. But in the heat of the argument neither Katy nor Sugar Man cared who was watching.

"Don't lay that sanctimonious crap on me Kat!" Sugar Man retorted angrily. "You are not Alice and this ain't Wonderland! You had to know what you were gettin' into here! Look at me girl! I'm a black man! Look at my clothes! What did you think I was a lawyer or somethin'? Look at where you are! Look at these people! This is real life to them! They don't pack up at the end of the night and go home to play with Barbie! So you thought you were just gonna come down here and take a walk on the wild side and not let any of it rub off on you, huh? Wrong little girl because whether you know it or not I'm under your skin! You want me bad! You think about me all the time! You lay awake nights wonderin' what it would be like to be with me...I know you do! You keep flyin' around me like a bee with some honey, the more you get the more you want! Admit it! You want me if for no other reason than to get back at *daddy* for not bein' the man you thought he should be and for hurtin' your little feelin's!"

Katy slapped Sugar Man hard across the face causing more of the crowd to turn and watch the ruckus. He let go of her arm and she ran out of the club and into the night. Sugar Man stood there rubbing the sting in his cheek and laughing as K.C. pushed past him and ran out after Katy.

Once outside the club, Katy ran straight into the old man that she remembered seeing outside Drake's apartment building. His sudden appearance frightened her and she grabbed her mouth to muffle a scream. The old man just looked at her woefully and simply asked, "Will you be made whole?"

"Katy," K.C. said as he touched Katy's shoulder, which did cause her to scream. She whipped around and relief washed over her as she realized it was K.C. and not Sugar Man.

"I'm sorry," K.C. said as he backed away from her slightly. "I saw what went down in there. Are you alright?"

Katy nodded as her eyes frantically searched for the old man who by then had disappeared.

"Can I give you a ride somewhere?" K.C. continued.

Katy was prepared to politely turn K.C. down but she thought better of it as she remembered that Sugar Man drove her to the club. "What about your *date*?" Katy inquired as she got into his car.

"I'll owe him!" K.C. laughed. "Besides I didn't really feel like being bothered with him anyway. Too messy!"

* * * * * * * * * *

"Where do you live?" K.C. questioned as he turned the key in the ignition.

"Evanston...Northwestern University," Katy responded as she buckled her seat belt.

"Northwestern University?" K.C. repeated with a puzzled look on his face. "I thought you..." K.C. stopped short of finishing his statement realizing that Katy was not who or what he thought she was. Katy was preoccupied with thoughts of Sugar Man and the scene in the club and the old man and the question he asked. "Will you be made whole?"

"That was pretty heavy back there," K.C. said trying to make conversation. "I mean back at *BISTRO'S* between you and Sugar Man. So he calls you Kat, huh?" he continued still not getting a response from Katy. "Kat!" he repeated. "It suits you!"

"Did you see that old man outside the club?" Katy asked oblivious to K.C.'s banter.

"Old man?" K.C. inquired. "Oh you mean Old Ben!"

"Old Ben," Katy repeated, finally putting a name behind his expressive and painful eyes.

"Don't let Old Ben scare you. He's a pretty harmless old dude," K.C. added. "He's always doing that. One minute he's there the next minute he's not. I remember when I first came to town, it seemed like everywhere I went he was there. He always had this way of just appearing out of no where. For a homeless dude Old Ben gets around. I'm tellin' you it used to freak me out. He was always talkin' about GOD and heaven and savin' my soul. After a while I just started ignorin' him and he just stopped botherin' me... You just ignore him; he'll eventually get tired and go bother somebody else.

It may have been easy for K.C., but Katy found it harder to ignore Old Ben and his pleading eyes. "Do you believe there is a GOD, K.C.?" she asked staring blankly out the window.

"I guess if you have to believe in somethin', GOD is just as good as anything else. Besides if there really is a GOD, He must have some sense of humor. Just look at the two of us!" K.C. quipped.

"Nothing seems to make sense," Katy mused.

When God Doesn't Make Sense. K.C. hadn't thought about that book in years. The conversation with Katy also brought back memories of a conversation he had several years before. "Have you ever seen the wind?" Elizabeth Goldberg asked him as they sat together on the Greyhound bus bound for Chicago. "You believe *it's* there, don't you?" As K.C.'s mind continued to wander he became more focused on what brought him to Chicago than driving the car.

"K.C. look out!" Katy shrieked as she braced for an accident. K.C. shook himself and swerved the car barely missing a small boy running in its path. The tires and brakes screeched to a halt and K.C. and Katy were thrust forward.

After collecting themselves Katy released her seatbelt and jumped out of the car to see about the boy. She ran over to the pile of garbage bags that the boy dove into to keep from being hit.

"Are you all right?" she asked as she tossed the bags aside.

"Get off me!" screamed the boy as he violently pushed Katy backward and darted off into the night.

K.C. had joined Katy by then and they both watched the boy disappear like a comet. Katy knelt down by one of the bags and picked up a cap that the boy had dropped. '*SPEED*' was the name stitched on the outside of the cap along side a decal of the Roadrunner.

After K.C. and Katy were sure that the other was all right they got back in the car. "Are you hungry?" K.C. asked looking at Katy.

"I'm starved!" she responded offering him a polite smile.

* * * * * * * * *

"You are not Alice and this ain't Wonderland! You had to know what you were gettin' into here! Admit it! You want me if for no other reason than to get back at *daddy* for not bein' the man you thought he should be and for hurtin' your little feelin's!"

Katy sat staring into the glass of water that the waitress poured and all she could think about was the severity of the truths that had come out of Sugar Man's mouth. She wanted him, which was apparent. His suave demeanor and the velvet like way in which his words caressed and seduced her. The way she tingled when his hot hands touched her skin. The way he looked. The way he smelled. The way his mouth formed when he said her name. Despite the fact that she now knew the heinous way in which he made his money, she still yearned for him, and he knew it.

"Earth to Kat...Hello is anybody in there?" K.C. playfully chided as he waved his hand in front of her. "You're thinkin' about Sugar Man ain't you?

"Is it that obvious?" Katy said as she pushed a plate of half-eaten French fries away from her.

"You seem like a nice girl Kat, and I'm the last one to offer anybody any advice..." K.C. began as he readjusted in his seat. "...but this is no place for you. You belong back at that university gettin' your education, not out here in the street playin' with fire. There's just too heavy a price to pay."

Katy listened to K.C. but she didn't hear him. Sugar Man's allure was too strong. He was dangerous and she knew it. She had to find a way to forget him. She had to make herself stay away from the flame.

11

Thelma Dennis, or Tee as she was called, had everything in her life to look forward to. Despite her impoverished urban surroundings she rose to become one of the top scholastic achievers at John F. Kennedy High School on the southwest side of Chicago. Tee had the brightest future of many of the other young women in her neighborhood. In spite of the fact that she had a five-year-old daughter, this 17-year-old 'A' student persevered. Tee had dreams of becoming a doctor. She had always had a fascination for anything to do with medicine. She loved watching medical dramas or documentaries on television. Biology, naturally was her favorite subject in school. However, in the summer of 1994, before her senior year Tee found herself pregnant again. Shortly after the birth of her son everything in her life spiraled, and she lost control of the grip that she once had on her stark reality. Tee's son Byron was born mildly retarded. Byron was a product of rape. A rape committed by Tee's 21-year-old brother Jerome.

Jerome was convicted and sentenced to 10 years in prison. Tee dropped out of school and stopped going to church. She couldn't stand being looked down on by "those saved folk." She became more social with some of the girls in and around her neighborhood who were considered "bad girls." She began to smoke and soon became addicted to crack cocaine. Her mother Rosetta, on the verge of a nervous breakdown, had only her faith and belief in GOD holding the fragile and battered pieces of her psyche together. Feelings of guilt and maternal failure prompted Rosetta to petition the court for custody of her grandchildren to keep social services from taking them away. One of the conditions of the judgment was that Tee was to stay away from her children until she had completed her court ordered drug rehab program. Two weeks into the program Tee dropped out.

In the span of a year Tee's entire personality was shattered because of what her brother had done to her. The once lively and energetic student ended up becoming no more than another statistic. Once majoring in Science and Biology the 18-year-old Tee found herself majoring in lying and stealing in order to support her habit. She also found herself pregnant for the third time.

* * * * * * * * *

"What in the world, " shouted the small wiry black woman as she rushed into her living room to discover her daughter rummaging through her purse. "I know good and well that you did not break in here and try to steal money from your own mama!"

"I didn't break in here," Tee countered. "I live here...and I wasn't tryin' to steal from you either. The kids knocked your purse on the floor while they were playin' and I was just pickin' it up!"

"You lyin' little crack headed fool...What do you take me for, huh!" Rosetta angrily retorted. "I swear girl if you don't get out of this house I'm gonna call the police!"

"POLICE!!!!" Tee shrieked. "You would call the police on your own daughter?"

"You would come in here and steal from your own mother?" Rosetta screamed. "Look I said it before, and since it didn't get through your dope filled head the first time I'll say it again...You ain't welcome in this house no more, do you hear me Tee!... I don't believe you! You were a good student and now look at you! You're pregnant again by some roughneck! You went and dropped out of school and got all messed up with that stuff... Lord Jesus!" Rosetta screamed throwing up her hands in defeat. "What did I ever do to deserve these hellish children?" She then charged at Tee, grabbed her by the arm and shook her. "You ignorant little tramp! Look at me Tee! Look at me!!!! I'm still young...I'm tryin' to have a life of my own and you and your kids are makin' it harder and harder for me! I'm only 36 years old and I look like I'm 50...You think I don't want a life, huh? You think I don't want a man! You think all I wanna do for the rest of my life is take care of these kids! When is it gonna be my turn, huh? When do I get to live? GOD help me before I lose my mind!!!"

"I didn't ask to be born!" Tee screamed as she pushed Rosetta away.

"AND I WISH YOU NEVER WERE!!!!" Rosetta shouted back as tears flowed down her cheeks. "Don't think for one minute you gonna drop another baby in this house either! The only reason they ain't all split up now is because I wasn't about to let social services come in here and take my grand babies. Ain't none of 'em got the same daddy. Brandy don't even know who her daddy is!"

"Well that makes us even then," Tee hissed. "Cause I don't know who my daddy is either! But we **both** know who Byron's daddy is don't we mama? He couldn't keep his hands off me and you knew it! You might as well have told him to do it!"

Unable to contain herself Rosetta slapped Tee in the mouth and in retaliation Tee slapped Rosetta back causing her to lose her footing and stumble into the sofa.

"You get out of here!" Rosetta screamed as she regained her balance. "You get out of here and don't you dare come back!"

* * * * * * * * *

Realizing what she had done Tee left her mother's house and went back to the shelter where had been staying since dropping out of rehab.

Most of her time Tee spent sleeping. When she wasn't sleeping she was out wandering the street looking for ways to score drugs. In fact her latest pregnancy came about as a result of a drug deal. She sold her body for the seduction of the crack pipe.

Tee never understood the allure of crack cocaine until she herself needed to find an escape. She tried to pray but the words just wouldn't come. She concluded that GOD didn't want to hear anything she had to say. She always thought of drug users as weak or stupid but as her life crumbled around her she became the thing that she had not understood.

When she first discovered that she was pregnant as a result of the rape she threw herself down a flight of stairs in the hopes of aborting the fetus. The only thing she succeeded in doing was breaking her arm. Tee's guidance counselor from school took a particular interest in her well being. She had been concerned about the changes in Tee's attitude as well as her grades. It was she whom Tee confided in. Mortified and unable to keep such a monstrous secret the guidance counselor reported the incident to the authorities. After Tee's brother Jerome was arrested a chain reaction of events began that contributed to the decline of a once bright and intelligent high school student who had, until that time, been able to overcome her surroundings and defeat her challenges. Despondent, bitter, and distraught Tee's only sanctuary was found in a glass vile.

12

Finals week was over. Katy's first semester at Northwestern had come to a close. Days had turned into weeks as Katy fought the urge to call Sugar Man. She didn't even tell Denise what she discovered about him. She didn't want to hear her say, "I told you so," so she kept quiet. But her silence turned against her. She was sure that because of her inability to concentrate she had not done well with any of her finals.

She thought about calling K.C. After all he had given her his number and told her to call anytime she wanted to. But K.C. was probably busy with Drake and all his other friends so she decided not to bother him. No longer able to resist, Katy picked up the phone. She dialed her father's number. The question in the back of her mind was what she would say to him if he answered the phone.

"Merry Christmas!" chimed a joyful female voice. Realizing it was her father's mistress, Katy slammed down the receiver. Despite how she felt she was going to be alone for Christmas just as she was for Thanksgiving. Before she left, Denise tried to convince Katy to come home to Indianapolis with her but Katy declined. So they simply exchanged gifts.

"Merry Christmas! See you next semester!" Denise shouted exuberantly as she headed out the door with her boyfriend Randy.

"Next semester," Katy lamented. It was all she could do to get through the first semester. She had not even begun to look forward to another one. She turned maudlin as she looked around the empty quiet room. She looked at the brightly wrapped present on her bed that Denise had given her and made her promise not to open until Christmas morning. But she was alone, she thought, who would know whether she waited or not. Katy's eyes lit up as she ripped open the box and pulled out a blouse that she had admired in the window of Marshall Fields weeks before. She stood in the mirror admiring herself when Ashley knocked at the door.

"Well it was nice knowing you!" Ashley said as she stood in the hallway all bundled up for the cold. "I just wanted to stop by before I left and give you this. I think you're going to need it." Ashley handed Katy and unwrapped bottle of gin. "Merry Christmas!" she said as she heartily embraced Katy.

Ashley had had a long talk with her mother and it turned out that she decided to leave Northwestern and return home to Champaign to try and work things out.

"I hope everything works out between you and your mom," Katy offered trying not to cry. Take care of yourself Ashley."

Katy stood in the hallway for several minutes after Ashley left listening to the deafening silence in the hallowed halls. Most of the students had gone home to family. Others had grouped up and went on skiing vacations or sought out warmer climates. But Katy was to spend the next several days alone with her thoughts and a bottle of gin.

She went back into the room and put a Christmas CD on and cranked up the volume. She grabbed the blouse and danced around the room singing loudly trying to drown out the loneliness. After several minutes of frolicking Katy jumped when she heard a loud pounding on the dorm room door. Without thinking she immediately turned down the volume and breathlessly answered the door.

Katy was stunned to find Sugar Man on the other side.

"Sorry about the pounding. I didn't think you could hear me over all that noise," he said.

Katy stood there staring at him in disbelief, breathing deeply, and trying to regain her composure. Her face was flushed from dancing and her clothes and hair were disheveled.

"Aren't you going to invite me in?" Sugar Man asked leaning casually against the door with his hands behind his back.

Katy offered no response as she nervously ran her fingers through her hair and straightened her clothes.

"You just gonna make me stand out here in the hallway after I drove all this way just to see you? Here I brought you something," he said as he presented a box from behind his back.

Katy reluctantly took the box from his hand and stepped back into the room. Sugar Man took slow and deliberate steps inside after her. As he removed his overcoat and gloves he looked around the room and smiled. "This is what I pictured your room to be like," he said as he looked at her and continued to smile. "Open the box," he encouraged. But Katy did not move. "Please," he whispered trying to effect sincerity.

Katy sat down at her desk and slowly opened the box. She gasped with delight despite herself as she realized what was in the box. Sugar Man had given her a kitten.

"I knew you'd like it," he said triumphantly. "What's this?" he continued as he spotted the bottle of gin. "Do you have any glasses? We could toast the holidays."

Realizing that she had never seen him drink anything other than coffee Katy glared at him in continued silence. Interpreting her look Sugar Man said, "It's a holiday!"

Sensing her resolve Sugar Man put down the bottle, picked up his coat and started towards the door. "I've missed you Kat," he said as he put on his coat. "I haven't been able to think about anything else for weeks." Sugar Man had his back to Katy but he could sense that he had struck a nerve and the ice was beginning to melt so he pressed on. "I hated the way we left things that night at the club. I said some hurtful things to you and if I could take them back I would."

Sugar Man reached for the door as he heard Katy say, "Don't go…Please…I don't want to be alone."

She couldn't see it, but Sugar Man flashed a chillingly evil grin, as he knew in that moment that he had won her over. Before he turned around to face her, he mouthed the word "Gotcha!"

* * * * * * * * *

The taxi drove onto the campus of Northwestern University and a wave of nostalgia swept over Kyle. It had been many years since he visited and the chance to make amends with his daughter offered him the perfect opportunity. Kyle rolled down the window of the taxi and took in the cold crisp air of December as he reminisced about the years he'd spent on the campus in the pursuit of higher learning.

Anxiety welled up in him as he approached Allison Hall. From the moment the plane touched down at the airport he'd rehearsed in his mind exactly what he would say to Katy to try and convince her to forgive him. "This is a time for family," he would say. "We need to work through our pain as best we can and move on." She must forgive him; he was not prepared to accept failure. Helen, the woman whom Kyle left Katherine for, encouraged him to make amends with his daughter because of the fact that he wanted to throw his hat into the political arena and run for public office in Ohio. Helen was good at spin control and she knew that Kyle's current estrangement from Katy would prove to be a public relations nightmare.

As Kyle slowly walked up the hall checking the room numbers against the paper in his hand he vacillated between assured victory and crushing defeat. As he got closer to the room number he was looking for the music that he heard since entering the building got louder. Kyle thought it was a little strange. The snow-covered campus appeared ghost like as he made his way through toward Allison Hall. He assumed that most of the students had already left for winter break. In fact he wasn't even sure that Katy would be there, still he had to try.

When he discovered that Katy's room and the source of the music were one in the same, trepidation overwhelmed him. What if she wasn't there? What if she'd decided to go elsewhere for the holidays? He had already decided what he would say to her but he could not predict what her response would be. He knocked — no answer. He waited for about half a second before he turned the knob of the door and opened it. As the light from the hallway flooded into the room Kyle was horrified. He could not believe what his eyes were seeing. His daughter was lying naked in the arms of a black man. His trepidation vanished and Kyle was immediately consumed with rage. "WHAT IN THE NAME OF ALL THAT IS HOLY IS GOING ON HERE!!!"

Katy was jarred by the thunderous sound of his voice and her eyes and mouth flew open simultaneously. She pulled the sheet that had barely covered her up to her face and cowered in fear. Sugar Man was not so easily intimidated by the looming figure of her father standing over them. He rolled over, yawned and stretched as if he were being awakened from a dream. Katy, on the other hand, felt that she had been flung directly into a recurring nightmare.

"Katy Jennings you get out of that bed this instant!" Kyle demanded as he turned away in shame.

Katy uneasily sat up on the bed as Sugar Man got up and swaggered over to Denise's bed to retrieve his pants.

"Dad what are you doing here?" Katy said embarrassed by his presence.

"No young lady," Kyle seethed. "I think the more appropriate question would be what exactly are *you* doing here?"

"Don't you think that's pretty obvious!" Sugar Man smirked as he pulled on his shorts.

Kyle looked at Sugar Man with murder in his eyes and charged at him. It proved to be a foolish mistake on Kyle's part given Sugar Man's stature and prowess. His reflexes were quick and deadly. He viciously slammed Kyle up against the wall and pinned his arm behind his back.

"Don't hurt him!" Katy screamed. As she bolted from the bed and tried to wedge herself between them.

Realizing his strength and the force that he had used to protect himself, Sugar Man backed off. Humiliated that he had taken such an uncalculated risk. Kyle shook the circulation back into his arm, removed a handkerchief from the inside pocket of his overcoat, and wiped the perspiration from his brow. Smoothing his hair back into place and straightening his clothes Kyle cleared his throat and demanded to speak to Katy alone. Katy looked pleadingly at Sugar

Man as if asking him to go. Sugar Man grabbed his leather overcoat, boots and the rest of his clothes, gently kissed Katy on the lips, winked at Kyle and left the room. The kitten that Sugar Man had bought for her pulled playfully at Kyle's pant leg. Katy bent down to pick up the kitten and turned off the CD player that had been playing the entire time. She put the kitten back in its box and walked over to her closet.

"Is this the kind of education Northwestern is dispensing these days?" Kyle demanded.

"No," Katy said as she dropped the sheet and pulled on her bathrobe. "Sugar Man is my extra credit assignment!"

"Don't be glib!" Kyle snapped. "*Sugar Man?*" he continued in disgust. "What kind of name is that!"

"Dad what are you doing here?"

"I came here to try and make amends," Kyle began. "I came here in an effort to try and restore some semblance of family between the two of us, but now I can see that that was a grave error on my part. I did not pay good money for you to come to this school and get mixed up with this, this *Sugar Man* character! Do you understand me young lady!"

"In case you've forgotten dad, I am 18 years old and you cannot tell me what to do or who I choose to do it with!"

"I have had just about enough of your insolence!" Kyle raged as he grabbed Katy's arms and shook her.

"Take you hands off me!" she screamed as she violently pulled away from him.

Kyle immediately flashed back on the time he had lost his temper with his son when he caught him in a similarly compromising situation.

"Very well then," he said backing down. "Next semester we'll register you at Ohio State or some other place, but I am not footing the bill for you to lay up here with some nig..."

"...Don't you dare say that word!" Katy shrieked.

"Get your things you're going back to Youngstown with me tonight!" Kyle insisted.

"I am not going anywhere with you!" Katy hissed

Sugar Man stood on the other side of the door and listened intently as the battle raged on between Katy and her father. He knew that in the act of making love to her he had become a part of her and she had become a part of him. He knew that he had emitted more than just his seed, he knew that he had transferred his spirit.

"What kind of a hold does this man have on you?" Kyle screamed in disbelief.

"He doesn't have any kind of a hold on me! He loves me!" Katy shouted back.

"Love!" Kyle said sarcastically. "You don't know the first thing about love!"

"Well maybe if you beat me within an inch of *my* life you could teach me!" Katy responded sharply.

Kyle stared in bewilderment at his daughter and realized that in the wake of her resolve this was a fight that he could not win. He also knew that if he intended to have any kind of political future he would need to get Katy as far away from Northwestern and *Sugar Man* as he could. "My plane leaves in two hours," Kyle began as he reached for the door. "If you're not at the airport by then you'll leave me no choice but to cut you out of my life. I can put up with your blame. I can tolerate your hatred. But I will not be subjected to your impudence not as long as I pay the bills around here. Be at the airport in two hours or I no longer have a daughter!"

Katy could hear the disappointment in her father's voice but she was adamant, she would not be bullied into returning to Youngstown and she would not be given an ultimatum. Sugar Man stood in the shadows at the opposite end of the hall and watched triumphantly as Kyle walked away from his daughter's room. "She's all mine now," he thought as Kyle stepped onto the elevator.

Katy stood silently in the center of her room as tears streamed down her face. "Goodbye daddy."

13

The traffic light changed from red to green but K.C. sat paralyzed behind the wheel of his mustang and didn't move. He sat remembering the look in Drake's cloudy hazel eyes as he informed him that he'd been diagnosed with the AIDS virus. His friend, his mentor, his lover was going to die and there wasn't anything he could do to stop it. Tears welled up in K.C.'s eyes at the thought of losing this man. How was he going to survive without the only person that had meant anything to him since he was 13 years old? The harsh and intrusive sound of a horn blasted through the turmoil in his mind jarring him back to his senses. K.C. looked up and saw that the traffic light had turned red again. He floored the accelerator and sped through the intersection causing chaos and pandemonium as cars from the opposite direction swerved and slid on the icy streets to avoid collision.

K.C. could not think of returning to their apartment on Lakeshore without him. He drove and drove until he ended up on the West Side of town at the home of his friend Cookie Spencer.

"Hey baby boy!" the tall slender black woman said excitedly as she opened the door to her apartment. "What brings you to this neck of the woods?"

K.C. stood shivering in the doorway of Cookie's apartment resisting the urge to double over in pain. Cookie instantly detected the seriousness of his mood and took his arm and pulled him into her apartment.

"Are you all right?" she said as she sat him down on the sofa. "I'll get you a drink," she said pulling her robe closed and moving quickly to the kitchen area of her one bedroom apartment. "I only have beer if that's O.K.!" she said as she popped the top and poured it into a glass. Cookie handed him the glass of beer and sat down on the love seat facing him. She took a cigarette from the pack that she had on her coffee table, lit it, sat back on the love seat, and waited patiently for K.C. to unburden himself. By his haggard look she could tell that he had not slept for some time. K.C. stared into the glass of beer and in one swift move turned it up and drank it down.

"You want another one?" Cookie asked.

K.C. remained silent. Instead he reached into the inside pocket of his leather jacket and pulled out a bag of marijuana.

"Now you're talkin'!" Cookie said as her eyes widened and she sat up on the edge of the love seat.

"Drake is in the hospital," K.C. said dully as he rolled his third *joint*. Cookie looked at him and then looked away as if she understood the pain she saw in her friend's eyes. Over the years she had lost more friends than she could count to this indiscriminate killer and now she needed to brace herself for more loss.

"What about you?" she asked quietly not really sure that she wanted to know the answer.

"I tested negative," K.C. responded as he lit the *joint*. "Drake's been sick off and on since before Thanksgiving. I had to take him to the hospital Christmas Eve. The doctors said it was pneumonia."

Cookie was more K.C.'s friend than Drake's. Unlike Drake, K.C. was not as exclusive when it came to the people that he chose to hang out with. K.C. first met Cookie when he was 16 and got into his first gay bar. He thought she was a kick to party with and she thought the same of him. Cookie said she was in her late twenties, but no one was ever able to pin down her real age because she looked younger. On the street working her trade, Cookie was rarely seen without her trademark pageboy-cut blonde wig. It was a way for her to shield her true self from public scrutiny. In this way she was anonymous; she was a fantasy; she was invisible. But in the solitude of her apartment the wig came off. She was able to divorce herself from that woman, if only for a time, and be herself. Sugar Man first hooked up with Cookie when he saw her stripping in a bar in St. Louis. She was instantly taken with the silver-tongued womanizer and after a torrid love affair she packed up and followed him to Chicago.

Cookie's relationship with K.C. was of a different sort. She immediately became protective of him, to her he was like the little brother that she never had. She took K.C. under her wing and "showed him the ropes." K.C. often objected to her instruction because he felt like he wanted to do his own thing. "You may be bigger than me..." she would jest, "...but I can still whip your narrow behind!" Drake didn't care much for Cookie because of her low life associations; she was Sugar Man's number one girl. Although Drake did business with Sugar Man he was more discriminating when it came to socializing with him. K.C. didn't care; Cookie was all right as far as he was concerned. She was a friend.

While Cookie sat trying to comfort K.C. there was another knock at her door. When Cookie went to open it she found Tee standing on the other side.

"Sorry to bother you" Tee began nervously, "but I was wonderin' if you could tell me where I can find Sugar Man?"

"Well he ain't here!" Cookie snapped putting one hand on her hip and holding the door ajar with the other.

"He was supposed to meet me down on the corner. I got money see!" Tee continued as she pulled a wad of crumpled dollar bills from her jean pocket while at the same time trying to peer over Cookie's shoulder to see who was in her apartment.

"Did you try lookin' down at the arcade or the pool hall?" Cookie continued as she stepped outside the door and pulled the door behind her.

"Uh...No...Maybe I'll try there! Thanks!" Tee said as Cookie stepped back inside her apartment and closed the door in her face.

"A year ago the child wouldn't hardly speak to me livin' right upstairs...," Cookie said as she walked back to the sofa. "Now the girl acts like we're best friends or somethin'."

Cookie looked and saw that K.C. had fallen asleep on her sofa. She went into her bedroom and retrieved a comforter and laid it gently across him and turned out the light.

"Lord!" she murmured as she stood in the darkness. "What next?"

14

With the Christmas holiday over 1996 was fast approaching. Katy was in her dorm room preparing to go to a party with Sugar Man. In spite of her father's demands, perhaps to spite him, she stayed at Northwestern and continued to see Sugar Man. Katy felt a little remorseful however that things were in such a state between her and her father. They were like two opposite magnetic forces trying to come together. At least he tried, Katy thought as she sat in front of her vanity mirror applying makeup. *She* should at least try to meet him half way. As the clock moved toward midnight she thought that she should give him a call.

"Hello," said the unfamiliar voice on the other end of the telephone.

"Hello," Katy responded hesitantly. "Is this Kyle Jennings' residence?"

"Yes it is," the female voice responded.

"May I speak with him please?" Katy inquired.

"I'm sorry Mr. and Mrs. Jennings are away on their honeymoon and I don't know when to expect them back.... Hello...Hello...Is anyone there?"

Katy hung up the phone and sat on the edge of her bed in disbelief. "He married her," she said as she picked up the kitten that Sugar Man had given her.

* * * * * * * * *

1996 did not hold much promise for K.C. either. Drake was still in the hospital as his condition steadily worsened. K.C. sat vigil at his bedside almost everyday waiting for some sign of recognition from him. Intravenous tubes ran out of Drakes arms, oxygen masks covered his nose and mouth, and monitors beeped and hissed indicating life. But to K.C. there was no life. This was not the man that he had come to know and love. This empty hollow shell was not Drake. It was all happening too fast K.C. thought. "Please God!" K.C. cried, "Don't do this!"

Drake had known for well over a year that he had contracted the AIDS virus but he didn't bother to admit it to K.C. Even when K.C. pressed him in regard to his health he would only laugh and tell him not to worry. As his symptoms progressed, Drake found it harder to conceal the physical changes that had begun to ravage his body. It seemed that from the time he admitted his plight to K.C. until the time he was admitted into the hospital, his condition rapidly deteriorated. And K.C. felt the need to take care of him.

"I want you to know something," Drake whispered to K.C. shortly after he told him that he had AIDS. "I love you."

Despite himself K.C. broke down and cried like a baby. The words sounded foreign to him. It had been so long since anyone told him that they loved him. Even his mother found it hard to make that confession after Warren entered the picture. K.C. tried to be strong in front of Drake and not show how much he was hurting but the reality was that Drake did love him. And it was a love that transcended his sexuality. Drake told K.C. years before that the reason he had shown so much concern for him when he found him beaten and bloodied in the bathroom of the Greyhound bus station was because he remembered what it had been like for him. A neighborhood gang had savagely attacked Drake when he was 11 years old. As a child his features were softer and more effeminate than those of other boys his age and older boys liked to harass him about it. They spoke to him and tried to pick at him in a manner as they would a girl and when he tried to fight back they raped and beat him.

* * * * * * * * *

Sugar Man rented out the Gemini to throw a party. Sort of a post Christmas pre New Years celebration. He handled the guest list and made sure there was plenty of everything that anybody wanted. He had even planned the entertainment. He sauntered into the club with Katy on his arm and flashed a wide toothy grin. Katy felt deliciously provocative dressed in the leopard print skintight low cut dress Sugar Man bought for her specifically for the occasion. He wanted to show her off, he wanted everyone to see her. Jealousy ate away at Cookie from the moment they made their grand entrance. Fire filled her eyes as she downed her third shot of tequila and watched the couple as they milled through the crowd.

"Who is this!" she seethed as they got closer to her.

The smile disappeared from Katy's face as she interpreted the bite in Cookie's tone.

"This is Kat," Sugar Man said as he signaled the waiter for a coffee. "Kat I'd like you to meet an old friend of mine... Cookie Spencer."

"Nice to mee ...," Katy extended her hand for an introduction.

"What ever!" Cookie snapped brushing Katy's hand away and turning away from them.

"Excuse us for a minute," said Sugar Man as he grabbed Cookie's arm and pulled her off the barstool and through the crowd.

Katy ordered a gin and ginger ale and watched the quarrel Sugar Man was having with Cookie at the other end of the bar. At one point it looked as if Cookie tried to slap him but he grabbed her hand. The look in Sugar Man's eyes sent chills through Katy. She'd seen that look before the day that her father tried to attack him in her dorm room.

As she continued to observe them Katy was interrupted by a husky bass voice from behind her. "Hey sweet thing what do they call you?" the man asked lewdly. Katy turned around to face him, all 360 pounds of him. "You must be new around here," he continued. "I've never seen you around before."

"I've been around," Katy said trying not to sound naïve as she sipped her drink.

"I know all of Sugar's girls and I definitely have never seen you before. I sure would have remembered if I had."

The leer in his eyes and his heavy lusty breathing made Katy feel as if she needed a bath. He pressed closer into her as he spoke and she tried to squirm free. A rush of relief came over her when she looked up and saw that Sugar Man was headed back in her direction. The overbearing stranger moved away from Katy and started toward Sugar Man. He stopped him halfway down the bar and began talking to him. They both looked at Katy and the stranger kept pointing at her and smiling. Sugar Man nodded agreeably as the exchange between the two continued.

Katy had a very uneasy feeling as the air suddenly felt thicker and the pulse of the music became unbearable. She put her glass down on the bar and pressed her way through the crowd and toward the door. Once outside Katy stood shivering in the cold as she took in one deep breath after another to clear her head. Though a bit blustery, it was a refreshing change from the way she'd began to feel inside the club. She closed her eyes and threw her head back and let out a sigh of relief. Suddenly as if out of no where she heard someone call "Katy." Her eyes sprung open and she looked around to see people coming and going but no one looked as if they had called her name. Besides, she thought, no one knew her here, so she dismissed it as if it were just her imagination. When she turned to go back inside the club she saw Old Ben standing at the opposite end of the corner. She was awestruck by his gaze and her heart sank. From where she stood he looked as if he was crying and she somehow could feel his pain.

"So this is where you ran off to," Sugar Man said as he came through the door. Katy jumped and stared blankly into Sugar Man's eyes.

"Who was that man you were talking to?" she asked.

"Oh you mean Earl? Earl is harmless!" Sugar Man offered. "He wanted me to apologize to you for making you feel uncomfortable."

Katy nodded lamely and looked back down to the street corner but Old Ben was gone.

"Come on back inside before you catch cold," Sugar Man said as he wrapped his arm around Katy and ushered her back inside.

When they got back inside they sat down at the table they had occupied when Katy first met Sugar Man. He signaled the waitress and within minutes she brought their order, gin and ginger ale for Katy and a coffee for Sugar Man. Katy slowly sipped the drink and a warm sensation quickly took the chill away.

"Is Cookie an old girlfriend or something?" Katy asked.

"Something like that," Sugar Man whispered as he nuzzled her cheek. "But you don't have to worry about Cookie," he continued as he gently kissed her on the lips. "You're my girl now."

Katy smiled as Sugar Man's seductive manner began to take affect on her.

"Your hair looks a little wind blown baby. Why don't you go and take care of that for me."

Like a sheep going to the slaughter Katy unsuspectingly got up and went to the ladies room. While she was gone Sugar Man went into action. Cookie, who was seated at the bar still reeling from their quarrel, watched as he slipped *flunitrazepam,* or *roofies,* as it is known on the street into the remainder of her drink. He looked up and saw that Cookie was watching him and he laughed.

* * * * * * * * *

Katy's nude body lay sprawled across the king-sized bed in the dimly lit motel room. She could only squint as she attempted to open her eyes. Her head felt like lead as she slowly lifted it from the pillow. All of her senses were still dulled somewhat as she began to rouse herself. When she tried to focus and figure out where she was she had to grab her head to keep herself from drifting back into unconsciousness. The air in the room was thick with the pungent aroma of marijuana. After a few more minutes of delirium she began to focus. The realization that she was naked and in a strange bed caused her to pull the sheets up to cover herself. A tremendous fear consumed her when she realized that she couldn't remember what had happened to her, how she got to the room, or why she was naked.

"Where are my clothes?" she thought as she pulled herself up to get out of the bed. She shuddered and jumped when she heard the sound of a toilet flushing in the adjacent room. A few seconds later Earl emerged from the bathroom. Katy gasped in horror when she saw that he was half-naked as well.

"Good mornin' sweet thing. You're up!" Earl said beaming.

"W...Where am I?" Katy asked clearing her throat.

"You're in a motel room with me!" Earl responded as he pulled on his shirt.

"What did you do to me?" Katy pressed, as her breathing became static.

"Nothin' that you didn't want to have done!" he responded dropping his friendly demeanor.

Nausea swept over Katy as she bolted for the bathroom. She gagged and retched at the terrifying thought of what might have taken place in that room. Things that she couldn't control. Things that she couldn't remember. She splashed water on her face and caught her reflection in the mirror. "Oh God!" she cried in agony, she barely recognized the image that stared back at her.

"Where are my clothes?" Katy demanded as she walked back into the room. By then Earl was fully dressed. He stood arrogantly by the window and nodded in the direction of the closet. As Katy moved to the closet Earl lit a cigar, sat down on the edge of the bed, and watched her. Katy grabbed her clothes and ran back into the bathroom and locked the door behind her. She turned on the shower as hot as she could stand it and stepped in. The water couldn't get hot enough to burn away the loathing she felt at the thought of Earl's fat hands touching her, or his obese body laying with her. She scrubbed and scrubbed until she wore herself out. Then she just collapsed into the tub and let the water pound her body. Several minutes later the water started to turn cold so she got out of the shower, dried herself off, and put on her clothes. The same clothes that she had worn to the club. The same clothes that made her feel provocative and sexy now made her feel smutty and cheap. She still felt naked, but there was no other covering for her so she had to wear what she had. After she was dressed, Katy lowered the lid on the toilet and sat down. She buried her face in her hands and cried profusely. She was startled when the handle on the door began to turn. She assumed that Earl was coming in after her and she frantically scanned the room for something to fight him off with.

"Kat! Kat it's me baby," she heard from the other side of the door. "Open the door Kat."

It was Sugar Man. Overjoyed to hear a familiar voice, Katy opened the door without thinking and flung herself into his arms. She looked around the room and noticed that Earl was gone. Suddenly she remembered that Sugar Man was the last person she was with. She violently pushed him away and stared at him as all things instantly became clear. All the signs she should have picked up on along the way. All the things she dismissed in her subconscious. Katy had been a willing pawn in his world, a world full of excitement and wonderment. She knew what kind of man he was but she was so blinded by his allure and appeal that she foolishly thought that he could never hurt her. Katy assumed that she was special to him, which was how he wanted her feel. She wanted to believe that he had genuine feelings for her but it was all a lie. Sugar Man had woven a cunning web of deceit and manipulation masked in charm and seduction. When she looked into his eyes she no longer saw the captivating gaze of a handsome stranger but the cold and evil stare of a monster.

"What did you do to me!" she screamed as she scratched and clawed at his face and drew blood.

Sugar Man grabbed her and sent her hurling against the wall. "The *cat* has claws!" he sneered as he removed a handkerchief from his leather overcoat and wiped the blood away. "Don't you ever...ever do that again! Do you understand me?" Katy lay whimpering on the floor as he removed money from his wallet and threw it at her. "Earl wanted me to give you a tip," he said softening his tone as he sat down in a chair near the window.

"You drugged me," Katy cried. "How could you do that to me? I thought you loved me!"

"I do love you Kat," Sugar Man whispered. "But it's my kind of love. You're my new number one girl."

Katy sat up and leaned against the wall. She looked around the room. She looked at Sugar Man. Then she looked at the money on the floor in front of her and laughed.

"For all your posturing," she began in disgust. "For all your Armani suits and all your charisma, you're nothing but a common drug dealing pimp! *Albert!*"

Sugar Man sat for a moment then he got up from the chair and slowly walked over to Katy. He crouched down and she drew away from him. He reached out to her and she turned away. "Kat, Kat, Kat...You wound me," he began as he entwined her hair in his fingers. "You should know by now that there is nothing *common* about me at all." As he said that he removed a manila envelope from his coat pocket and pressed it into her hand. "Happy New Year baby," he said as he got up and returned to his chair.

Reluctantly Katy opened the envelope and pulled out its contents. There were pictures of her and Earl together in that very room having sex. Katy was repulsed. She furiously ripped the pictures into pieces.

"I have the negatives!" Sugar Man announced triumphantly. "How do you think the Dean of Students at that university of yours would react to getting copies of those pictures? Better yet how do you think *daddy* would react? Even better how much do you think he'd pay to keep these pictures out of the public eye?"

Katy was mortified. She slowly picked herself up off the floor, grabbed her coat and purse and left the room. She left the torn pictures and the money on the floor and she left Sugar Man sitting in the chair and just walked away. She walked out onto the streets of Chicago in a daze. She had no idea where she was or how she was going to get back to Evanstown. She riffled through her purse and could only find ten dollars and change. The cold and brutal wind of the city whipped through her cashmere overcoat like shards of glass but she kept walking. She stopped at a newsstand long enough to read the headlines of the Tribune. "December 31st," she said out loud. She'd lost an entire day. When she turned around she came face to face with Old Ben. She stood there for a moment thinking that he would just disappear again but he did not.

"Who are you?" she questioned. "Why do you keep showing up all over the place?"

"I was trying to help you before you fell in," Old Ben firmly stated meeting her stare. "Now it's my job to help you get out."

"Paper lady?" inquired a small voice from behind her.

Katy turned around and looked into the small radiant face of a ten-year-old boy. Katy remembered seeing him once before the night that she and K.C. almost ran him over. "Speed," she said silently.

"You want a paper?" he repeated. "Or can I sell you something else?" he said opening his backpack to reveal several small envelopes and plastic pouches. "Drugs," Katy thought shaking her head.

She turned around and once again Old Ben was gone. She looked up at the street sign and saw that she was standing on the corner of State Street and Roosevelt Road. How was she supposed to get back to the university from here? She looked across the street and there she saw a diner. She made her way across and went in. She scanned the room for an available table and noticed K.C. sitting with his head down in the corner.

"Kat," he said as he looked up into her face. "What are you doin' here?"

Katy looked into K.C.'s stricken face and she was instantly moved with compassion. His eyes were bloodshot from crying and his nose was as red as hers.

"Are you all right?" she asked sympathetically.

"No," he responded as he sat up and fell back into his seat. "But I will be."

He invited Katy to sit and at her request he began to unburden himself. Katy sat and listened empathetically as tears filled her eyes. She reached across the table and took his hand to comfort him. She had forgotten all about her problems and the last 24 hours in the wake of what K.C. had revealed.

"Drake died at 4:30 this morning," K.C. said quietly. "He just went to sleep and never woke up."

Unable to help herself Katy heaved and let go of her tears. K.C. soon found himself comforting her. Realizing that they were making an emotional spectacle of themselves K.C. suggested that they leave and go back to his apartment on Lakeshore Drive.

Embarrassed by the way she was dressed Katy kept her coat pulled tightly around her. K.C. instinctively knew that something had happened with her and that something somehow involved Sugar Man.

* * * * * * * * *

When they got to his apartment K.C. offered Katy a pair of sweats to change into. She graciously accepted and asked if she could use his shower, even though she knew that no amount of soap and water was going to be able to wash away the dirt she felt inside her soul. When Katy went in to take her shower K.C. stood silently in the center of the living room and closed his eyes. Pickles came out from her hiding place and wrapped herself around his legs. He bent down to pick her up and went into the kitchen to get her some food. When he returned to the living room he walked over to the fireplace and looked at all the pictures he and Drake had taken together over the past seven years. He picked up the last picture they had taken together at the Taste of Chicago in July the year before he started getting sick. The anguish that he felt caused K.C. to double over. As he sat on the floor in a heap he felt a hand touch him on the shoulder. Katy sat quietly down beside him and held him in her arms and allowed him to grieve.

As the clock struck midnight signaling the start of the New Year, K.C. and Katy sat on the floor of the 22nd story high-rise looking for a way to cope with what lay ahead for them both.

15

Drake requested to be cremated and that his ashes were to be scattered from atop the Sears Tower overlooking the city that he loved. The arrangements for Drake's cremation were provided for by a funeral director he had been in contact with months before his death. The news of his impending death caused an uproar among his clientele. With Cookie's help, K.C. arranged a quiet memorial service for his friend. During his illness and especially after his death K.C. discovered who Drake's friends really were. Drake kept a coded log of all his most important and influential customers and K.C. contacted all those he considered to be among Drake's closest associates but none of them returned his phone calls. In fact several of them changed their numbers. K.C. even called Drake's mother who lived in Michigan. She and Drake had had little or no contact over the years because she could not accept his lifestyle and was unwilling to accept his death. She flatly refused to come to his memorial.

Drake's memorial was held at the Gemini Club. The Gemini was the place Drake sometimes referred to as his second home because he spent so much time and money there before he died. In honor of his passing, the club's proprietor decided to close the club long enough for the service to be held.

From the time she debuted on the Broadway stage, Jennifer Holiday had become Drake's favorite female vocalist. He had all of her albums and boasted that he'd seen 'Dreamgirls' at least 20 times, in New York alone. As the guests assembled inside the club the irony of her dynamic and powerful rendition of 'And I Am Telling You I'm Not Going' filled the room. If everybody Drake had partied with over the years had shown up the place would have been filled to capacity but fear kept them away. As it was only about 40 people were in attendance.

Cookie watched over K.C. with the fierceness of a mother hen. She barely tolerated Katy's presence. But she knew that K.C. wanted her there. Cookie had not let go of the fact that it was Katy who had taken her place in Sugar Man's life. Cookie believed as Katy had, that she meant something to this man. But that's how Sugar Man had planned it all along. That was the way he operated. He made you believe, and then he beguiled you with his crafty ways and charming demeanor. They couldn't see that a man with no heart could never have a soul.

One by one the varied mourners got up to speak and recount their most endearing memories of Drake Sommersbee, but K.C. gave the most moving eulogy of all. He shared stories that made laughter and tears flow equally throughout the room.

"What I will always remember about Drake," K.C. began resisting the urge to cry. "Is that he was compassionate. He found me when I was at the lowest point in my life and he made it possible for me to live again. He loved me. He never judged me. He never used me. He was my friend."

Silence fell over the room as K.C. returned to his seat. Cookie stood to embrace him and Katy embraced him as well. Suddenly the tender moment was disrupted when Sugar Man entered the room. Otis and some other men in the room got up to stop him but he pushed them aside. He approached the table where K.C. was and blew a kiss in Katy's direction. She looked at him with contempt and turned away. Cookie instinctively jumped to K.C.'s defense.

"Sugar don't come in here startin' nothin'," she said under her breath. "Not today!"

"I don't wanna start nothin'," he responded sounding half-sincere. "I just came to pay my respects."

Cookie cautiously sat down and Sugar Man proceeded to K.C. "Now that your *free ride* is dead," he said quietly so that no one heard him but Cookie, and Katy. "There's always a place in my organization for a pretty thing like you."

K.C. lunged at Sugar Man and punched him in the mouth almost knocking over the urn that held Drake's ashes. Cookie and Katy both leapt to assist K.C. as Sugar Man over powered him and flung him across the room. K.C. knew that with his karate training he could have easily done some damage to this loathsome excuse for a human being but he didn't want this solemn occasion to be marred by any further violence so he backed away. Having caused the disturbance that he set out to do, Sugar Man straightened his clothes and left the bar.

* * * * * * * * *

After Drake's ashes were scattered and they saw Katy safely on a train back to Evanston, K.C. and Cookie returned to his Lakeshore apartment to find yet another surprise awaiting them. Government agents had seized all the property under the name of Drake Sommersbee; a.k.a. David Slaughter; a.k.a. Derrick Simpson; to auction. Drake had diversified quite a few of his holdings into several different accounts under several different aliases with several different social security numbers. It seems that the government tracked him down based on discrepancies in his tax reporting. But their timing could not have been worse. K.C. was not allowed to re-enter the apartment to retrieve anything that belonged to him. He had to leave all of his music, all of his clothes, and all of his memories. As far as the government was concerned what ever they seized became their property, even the car that Drake had given him. Not willing to risk a fight for fear that his true identity would be revealed, and with only a few hundred dollars in his pocket, K.C. walked away. This was the second time in his life that K.C. had to walk away and leave everything behind. This was the second time in his life that his future was bleak and uncertain and there was no telling where he would end up this time. After settling in with Cookie, K.C. attempted to withdraw money from the joint account he shared with Drake. He discovered that along with everything else, the government had confiscated all Drake's accounts. "You will get through this," he thought as he and Cookie boarded the "L" and headed back to her place. "You will get through this."

* * * * * * * * * *

By the time Katy returned to Allison Hall she discovered that Denise had returned from winter break. Denise was all smiles and full of conversation about her family and her boyfriend.

So much had happened to Katy since Denise left that she was far beyond hearing how things were going in her 'perfect world'. Denise noticed right away the distinct changes in her roommate and thought it best that she not push for conversation.

"I know things can get a little rough," Denise said trying to lighten the mood in the room. "But when did you take to eating cat food?"

Katy looked at Denise and saw that she was holding up a box of food that she bought for the kitten.

"Don't tell me you brought a cat in here!" Denise grimaced.

Katy told Denise that she had been given a kitten for Christmas but that she gave it away. Denise didn't know what to make of Katy's strange behavior so she shrugged it off thinking it had to do with her father. Katy changed from the blouse and slacks that she had worn to the memorial into a pair of jeans and the oversized sweatshirt that K.C. had given her. "There!" she thought as she fell back on her bed feeling like the old Katy. She rolled over to her nightstand and there among her papers she found the red ribbon that her brother Kyle had given her when she was nine. She wrapped it around her fingers, whispered his name, and got misty. The sound of the phone ringing broke her sullen mood, but she made no attempt to answer it.

"Aren't you going to answer it?" Denise asked. Realizing that she wasn't, Denise put down the clothes that she was putting away, huffed, and picked up the phone.

"Hello!" Denise said impatiently. "Kat? Sorry there's nobody named Kat here. You have the wrong...Oh well why didn't you say so!"

Denise put the receiver to her chest and whispered to Katy, "It's a man for you. It sounds like he's been crying."

Assuming that it was K.C., Katy reached for the telephone. Once she said hello she realized she had been duped.

"Hey baby," Sugar Man said seductively. "I wouldn't hang up the phone if I were you," he continued hurriedly. "That is if you don't want me to come there and turn that fine little roommate of yours onto our little party."

Sugar Man got Katy's full attention. He talked and she listened. Sugar Man told her what he expected her to do to keep the pictures of she and Earl from becoming public. Tears streamed down her face as he spoke. Fear and intimidation collided inside her causing Denise to take notice and become worried. Without saying a word Katy buried her face in her pillow and sobbed uncontrollably.

"Please Katy...Talk to me...Tell me what's wrong?...Tell me what I can do to help?" Denise asked sensing Katy's anguish.

Katy felt trapped. There wasn't a thing that anyone could do. As long as Sugar Man had something over her she would continue to play his game by his rules.

16

"Mama, it's me, Tee. I'm in jail… They lied mama…They say I was shopliftin' but I wasn't mama I swear! Can you please come and get me out? Please mama, I need help! Don't let me stay in here! I promise I'll get it together. I promise I'll get clean. I promise I'll go back to school, just please come and get me."

Tee made one empty promise after the other and Rosetta reluctantly helped her every time. How could she not? Tee was her daughter and she knew deep down that if her son hadn't done what he did, Tee wouldn't have fallen into such deep despair. Guilt and shame tormented Rosetta day and night. But it wasn't the guilt of the present. It was the guilt of the past that kept her locked in her own private hell. The hell, Rosetta lamented, that would make her pay penance for the rest of her life. Rosetta heard a sermon once concerning generational curses but it wasn't until her son Jerome raped his sister that she believed that they existed. This was not the first time that the scourge of incest had been visited upon her family. It was shame that kept Rosetta from dealing with the truth. And that same demonic force that tried to destroy her had come back and destroyed her daughter.

Try as she might Rosetta was unable to handle Tee's crack addiction. As much as she felt for her daughter's condition she couldn't allow her to stay in her house, and she couldn't allow her to negatively influence her granddaughter Brandy.

The insidious enticement of the crack pipe held Tee hostage and she became insatiable. The temptation was too strong and Tee was unable to resist the urge to succumb to its power.

* * * * * * * * *

Katy did all she could to ignore Sugar Man's relentless pursuit, including changing her phone number, but he would not give up. Sugar Man finally forced a confrontation when he showed up on the university campus one day and tracked her down. He followed her from one class to the next until he'd worn down her resolve.

"If you don't leave me alone I'm going to have campus security lock you up!" she screamed.

Undaunted, Sugar Man laughed, "Go on! I dare you!"

"Why are you doing this to me?"

"Because you belong to me now!"

Their encounter was attracting a lot of undo attention from students and faculty members alike but none dared approach them. Katy knew that she would not be able to continue in this manner much longer. She knew that she would soon have to make a decision as to what to do.

* * * * * * * * *

Well over a month had passed since Drake's memorial. With no where else to go, Cookie invited K.C. to stay with her. Having none of the trappings that he had become accustomed to with Drake, K.C. found himself working the streets to make enough money just to survive. Sex was a commodity that was in high demand, the better you were, the more money you made. With Drake as his mentor K.C. learned his craft well. He also found that he had adjusted rather well to smoking crack for a high in the absence of genuine cocaine. And until he discovered that she was pregnant, Tee had been his running buddy in the pursuit of the almighty *rock*.

"Hook me up!" Tee said as K.C. opened the door to Cookie's apartment. "Hook me up man! I know you got what I need! You got what I need baby!"

"Tee I told you to stop comin' around here," K.C. said as he tried to close the door on her. "I ain't got nothin' for you!"

"C'mon man you are the only friend I got," Tee continued as she pressed against the door. "I would go see Sugar Man but he wants too much money!"

"Tee you're pregnant! You should have been off this stuff a long time ago! You need to go back home and take care of yourself, and this baby! You're not as tough as you want people to think you are. You're just scared that's all. Why are you gonna mess up this baby's life before it even gets here?"

"I don't give a rip about this baby!" Tee snapped. "What kind of a life is it gonna have anyway? I live in a halfway house not on Lakeshore Drive. You want it! You can have it! I just want a *rock* that's all! Besides, I got it all planned out...Just as soon as this thing comes out I'm gonna sell it and get some real money. Plenty of women out there that want kids and can't have none...Plenty!

"Tee nobody is gonna want a crack baby from a crack head!" K.C. chided.

Tee took offense to K.C.'s remarks and cursed at him as she walked back down the hallway to leave the building. As she left Tee ran directly into Old Ben.

"Hey Old Ben!" she said pulling her coat closed to shield herself from the cold. "Gimme some money! I know you got money! Carrying all those cans around all the time you must have plenty of money!"

Old Ben turned to her with a fierce look in his eyes and said vehemently, "Isaiah 42:22 says... This is a people robbed and spoiled. They are all of them snared in holes, and they are hid in prison houses. They are for a prey, and none delivereth; for a spoil and none said, RESTORE!"

Tee looked at him blankly and responded, "Aw man you buggin' with that ol' bible mess...If you didn't have no money that's all you had to say!" She then turned away from him and walked up the street asking each passerby for any change that they could spare.

As Tee disappeared up the block Old Ben turned toward the apartment building and saw K.C. standing in the window looking down at him. The intense gaze in Old Ben's eyes made K.C. back away from the window. As he did he heard Old Ben yell, "Restoration is coming for you too!"

It had been easy to dismiss Old Ben as a derelict before, but something inside K.C. was stirred now. He was beginning to see in his eyes the thing that Katy had seen and it deeply disturbed him.

17

"You were always the strong one." Those words haunted Katy again as she faced what she felt were the insurmountable odds against her. Katy agonized over whether or not she would be able to face herself much longer, much less be strong enough.

She closed her eyes tight and tried to remember a time when she believed she still had a family. She recalled she and her brother's seventh birthday. Kyle Sr. had taken the family to Disney World to celebrate. They were all happy then. Everything was as it should be. Her mother was vibrant and beautiful and full of life, and when Kyle Sr. looked at her, he still seemed to love her. But as Katy lay flat on her back staring at the ceiling of the clandestine hotel room, straining and trying to hold her breath, the memory of that happy time was obliterated by the reality of her present condition. Tears streamed down her face as she allowed her motionless body to be defiled.

Lack of money and the inability to contact her father caused Katy to give in to Sugar Man's extortion and she met with a "customer" that he'd set up. She thought that if she relented and did what he wanted her to do maybe he would have mercy on her and let her go. But one time became another, and then another, and then another until she was in so deep she felt she would never be able to get out. Self-recrimination and self-loathing tore away at her resolve little by little. She was caught in a spider's web of emotional and physical abuse that she was unable to free herself from.

When the nameless, faceless interlopers finished their debauchery they would leave their money and slither quietly back out into society. At first Katy wondered what kind of animal would get enjoyment out of paying for sex. But after her emotions started to die she convinced herself she didn't care. For all she knew these men could have wives and children waiting for them at home, or they could have been business men, lawyers, doctors, or just sick perverts who had enough money for a one night stand with a whore.

"Where do you disappear to at night?" Denise asked as Katy attempted to slip back into the dorm room unnoticed.

Katy would never answer. Though she wouldn't talk about it, Denise knew that the drastic changes in her roommate's behavior had something to do with her involvement with Sugar Man. Denise recalled the first time she looked into his eyes. That was the night that she and Ashley and Katy decided to play grown-up. Denise interpreted the look in his eyes as cold and unfeeling, she knew that nothing good would come of Katy's relationship with him. The more she objected the more Katy was drawn to him so eventually she stopped mentioning him altogether. After all, Denise reasoned Katy was a big girl and was more than capable of taking care of herself, at least that's what she told her.

Katy cried herself to sleep night after night and kept hoping that she would be dead before morning. But it never happened and the cycle continued. In spite of everything, Katy managed to hold on until winter began to give way to the first thaw of spring. But she knew that she could no longer continue to perform as the student-hooker. Because she was unable to concentrate on her studies long enough to maintain her GPA, Katy knew that she was headed for academic probation so she rationalized that school would have to go.

When Denise left for spring break, Katy prepared to move out of the dorm. She wrote Denise a goodbye note thanking her for her kindness and wishing her well. When they had finished filling the trunk of the car that K.C. borrowed to help her, Katy took one last look around the room, "Goodbye Katy Jennings," she whispered as she closed the door to her dreams. By then K.C. knew all about the pressure that Sugar Man used against

Katy to push her up against the wall. He was powerless however to do anything to help her stop him, and he was unable to find the words to convince her to stay in school. Given his own circumstances, K.C. was not convinced that he wouldn't have done the same thing if he were in her place. Together they found an apartment close to Cookie's building and with some second hand furnishings set up house.

It was definitely going to take some adjustment. For the most part the people on Madison Street kept to themselves. No one wanted to find themselves on the wrong side of a bullet. Not only did the occasional gang or drug related incident take some getting use to but it was unclear whether the police that frequented the neighborhood were there for business or pleasure. Sugar Man offered Katy an opportunity to live with him but she vehemently declined.

"I'd sooner die before I lived with you!"

'Fine then! Stay here with your little punk friend and the roaches! See if I care!"

Sugar Man lived near the Hyde Park area and Katy had been invited there on more than one occasion. She realized, although she would never give him the satisfaction of admitting it, that staying in his house would have been preferable to living in that neighborhood. But she wasn't about to turn her back on K.C., and between the two of them that was the best they could afford. K.C. made out all right but his services did not command the money that they once had. And as far as Katy was concerned, Sugar Man only gave her enough money to keep her in line. He couldn't take the chance that she would run.

* * * * * * * * *

Shortly after they settled into their new apartment, Cookie decided to throw K.C. a party to celebrate his 21st birthday. Though she was reluctant, she solicited Katy's help in the preparation. In a way Cookie actually felt sorry for the predicament that Katy was in. She knew that at least she had a choice when it came to doing what Sugar Man wanted, but Katy never had that choice. "The stupid little girl never knew what hit her," Cookie mused as she shared her tale with the bartender at Gemini's.

Cookie invited everybody to come and celebrate with K.C. Admittedly this was not the kind of party that he'd been used to with Drake, still he appreciated Cookie's efforts. The one good thing about the party was that Sugar Man did not bother to darken the place with his nefarious presence and K.C. was glad about that as was Katy. The party lasted into the wee hours of the next morning until the last of the revelers decided to go. Katy and Cookie helped K.C. gather all the gifts that he received and they too finally headed for home. They hailed a taxi, and by the time they'd gone two blocks Cookie was fast asleep. K.C. laid his head on Katy's shoulder, yawned and quietly said, "Thank you." Katy offered a slight smile but she was wide-awake. The thought of being free of Sugar Man's sadistic grip plagued her the entire night. As the taxi drove steadily through the burgeoning Sunday morning traffic Katy gave voice to her plan. "K.C.," she said softly. K.C. acknowledged her with a slight groan as she continued. "Have you ever thought about what it would be like to kill somebody?" With his head still on her shoulder, K.C.'s eyes opened as the seriousness of her tone grabbed his attention. He knew that she was referring to Sugar Man and it made him uneasy.

* * * * * * * * *

After the taxi dropped Cookie off and K.C. walked her to her door, he and Katy walked the rest of the way to their apartment. Katy was morose as they walked and barely said anything to K.C.

"I killed a man once," K.C. said calmly. Katy was the only other person he had told besides Drake. Cookie didn't even know that K.C. was more than just a runaway.

His admission took Katy by surprise and she looked at him in disbelief. The pace of their walk slowed almost to a halt.

"My stepfather," K.C. continued not looking at her. "I was 13 years old. I shot him… He killed my mother and I shot him, then I ran. I never looked back. It was the scariest thing I ever did."

The two stopped outside their apartment building and K.C. turned to Katy and said. "Kat I know what you're thinkin', and even if you get away with it you'll still never be free of him. He'll haunt you more dead than he did when he was alive."

The sinking reality of K.C.'s words struck Katy. She surmised that K.C. was talking about more than what she planned to do to Sugar Man. She looked at her friend and saw the haunted look in his eyes and she knew that he was talking about himself. She shifted the package that she had under her arm and took his hand giving it a gentle squeeze. A crooked smile formed in the corner of K.C.'s mouth and he nodded his head in the direction of the building and they went in.

Unable to sleep K.C. and Katy stayed up and watched the sunrise. Katy opened up to K.C. about her brother and mother's suicide, her turmoil with her father, and how she hated him for turning away from her every time she needed him to be there. K.C. too opened up and shared his life with Katy. They both talked and laughed and even cried about their individual tragedies until they exhausted themselves and fell asleep. Each of them dreamed about what life would have been like...if only.

18

Katy sat on the park bench and watched in amazement as Speed slyly made one dope transaction after another. She shook her head incredulously as she wondered how someone so young and so seemingly innocent could be caught up in such unscrupulous activity. But she knew first hand how far reaching Sugar Man's grasp could be. Speed did not lack customers either. And who could suspect a boy so young, and one that looked so harmless.

"Hey Kat," Speed said as he sat down on the bench next to her. "Want a hit?"

Katy shook her head as she asked; "Does your mother know that you're out here?"

"Yeah!" he responded sharply. "Why do you think I'm out here?...Does your mother know you're out here?"

Katy turned away from him as she felt the bite of retaliation. Out of the corner of her eye she saw Speed remove a big wad of cash from his pocket and count it.

"Soon as I give Sugar Man his cut I can buy that bike that I want!" Speed declared.

"Speed" was the only name that anybody ever called the child pusher. He was called Speed because he always ran everywhere he went. Everybody in the neighborhood thought that one day he would grow up to become a track star but Speed never had any dreams or aspirations that gave him hope of doing anything beyond what he was already doing. He had three sisters, and he was the self-proclaimed "man of the house." There had always been other men in and around the house but none that were capable of providing for his family. He never knew his father. When he was 9 years old his mother, who stayed at home collecting welfare checks, started *seeing* Sugar Man. It was Sugar Man that turned her on to smoking crack. Speed even assumed that his youngest sister, Sasha, was a product of their illicit affair. Sugar Man convinced his mother that Speed could make some real money running drugs for him and that he would be less conspicuous and she agreed. When Speed realized all the things he could buy for his mother, his sisters, and for himself, he was more than happy to comply. Speed was even glad that he had Sugar Man's protection from the gang members that continually taunted him. No one dared mess with Speed as long as they knew that they would have to answer to Sugar Man.

As Speed stuffed the wad of bills back into the pocket of his dirty jeans Katy's ears were tantalized by the melodic sound of music lingering in the breeze from the church on the corner. She had heard the music before in the month since she came to live with K.C., and she had seen the droves of people that flocked in and out of the sanctuary every Sunday and twice during the week. She had always been curious, but never curious enough to investigate. It was Easter Sunday, she thought to herself, and for some reason she now felt the courage to take a closer look.

It wasn't a very big church but it was large enough for Katy to feel trepidation as she walked up the street toward the edifice. As she got closer the music got louder she could hear voices interspersed with the music and she shivered with excitement. She changed her mind a hundred times as she ascended the stairs toward the door. She stood outside the church and closed her eyes as she heard the words to the music. *Amazing grace how sweet the sound that saved a wretch like me. I once was lost but now I'm found, was blind but now I see.* Lost. That's exactly how she felt. This must be a place that will be able to help her see her way more clearly she thought as she opened the door.

There were a few people standing in the foyer of the church as Katy timidly stepped inside. Their eyes widened and locked on her as if she sought to do them harm. She pulled nervously at the hem of her short skirt and clutched the collar of her jacket to close it over the low cut neckline of her blouse. One of the ushers reluctantly handed her a program and opened the door that led into the main sanctuary. Katy felt like a freak on display at a carnival as everyone near the door turned and watched her enter. Undaunted she pressed her way in and found a seat in the back. There was a man seated at the end of the pew that eyed her from head to toe, and then a woman who apparently was his wife poked him in his side and signaled for him to move away from her. Katy smirked as she thought that this could easily have been one of the many nameless *johns* that she had entertained over the last few months. She took a deep breath and reprimanded herself for having such a thought in church. As she sat she continued to observe how nice and colorful all the people looked. She hadn't given much thought to the way she was dressed until she sat down in the sanctuary and felt the penetrating stares of the congregation. What she wouldn't give for a baggy sweatshirt and a pair of jeans at that moment. A row of teenaged girls, not much older than her, pointed and giggled causing her to squirm and become more uncomfortable. One stern look from an usher and the girls quieted and turned back to face the front of the church.

"Amen!" the robust preacher shouted as he took his place behind the podium when the choir finished singing. "This is the day the Lord has made. Let us rejoice in it and be glad!"

Katy jumped nervously as the assembly riotously responded to the preacher's words.

"Do we have any visitors here with us today?" he asked as he scanned the room with welcoming arms.

Several people stood to their feet to be recognized and thunderous applause erupted throughout the congregation. Katy thought that that was a wonderful response to being recognized as a visitor so she too stood to her feet.

"Amen!" injected the preacher. "C'mon church let's show our visitors how much we're glad to have them with us today!"

Katy felt invisible as they all got up and went out of their way to avoid her as they hugged one visitor after the other, but no one approached her. Her heart sank. As the congregation returned to their seats she too sat back down. As the preacher delivered his message Katy took note of all the wonderful and powerful things that he said. He spoke of salvation and restoration and forgiveness of sin, but the word that stuck out to her most was love. Her eyes clouded with tears as he talked about love. Real love. GOD's love. But Katy didn't hurt because of his words; she hurt because nobody in the church exhibited any of the attributes that he described as love. She hurt because she couldn't even find refuge in GOD's house. Unable to take it any longer Katy jumped up from the pew and ran out of the church.

Katy ran back to the park bench across the street from her apartment building and sat down. She closed her eyes and took slow deliberate breaths as she berated herself for thinking that she had the right to walk into the church in the first place. "If Jesus makes you act like those people," Katy thought to herself, "they can keep Him because I got enough problems!" "Resurrection Sunday!" she sneered.

"The eyes of the Lord are in every place beholdin' the good and the bad," Old Ben said as he sat down next to Katy on the bench.

Startled Katy jumped up from the bench and stared at Old Ben as if he were a ghost. "You scared me!" she gasped. "Why are you always sneaking up on people?"

"I wasn't sneakin'," he said with a twinkle in his eye. "I was here the whole time."

"Yeah?" Katy sneered. "Then why didn't I see you then?"

"Because you weren't lookin'," he said as he gazed into her face.

Katy's throat went dry and a chill ran down her back. For some inexplicable reason she found it hard to break his gaze.

"This place is a long way from Ohio ain't it?" Old Ben asked in a way that suggested he knew the answer. Katy was alarmed by his disclosure but she was intrigued by his tone.

"Kind of makes you wish you never left home don't it?" Old Ben pressed. Hardly worth all the pain you left behind... You've been hurt, but you want to believe in somethin'. Why don't you take a chance on GOD? Nothing else has worked for you. You're dying out here in these streets. Nothing good can come of this life."

"I don't know anything about GOD, Ben," Katy snapped, "and apparently He doesn't know anything about me either!"

"He knows you've been hurt!" Old Ben continued. "He knows you have a problem with trust."

Katy looked down the street in the direction of the church and said sadly that she didn't want anything to do with a GOD that made you act like the people in the church.

"Don't look at the people Kat! Look at GOD! He's the only one that matters." Old Ben admonished. Again his tone and the words that he spoke moved Katy. There was something more to this man that sat with her on the park bench in his ragged moth eaten clothing and his dirty face wrapped in a heavy wool coat on a beautiful spring day. Who was he? How could he know anything about her? This mysterious gentle vagrant with the piercing eyes and knowing words. What was the message that he was trying to convey? Curiosity led Katy to test him further.

"Why are you always talking about GOD?" Katy asked as she joined him on the bench. "Look at you, you're a bum! You stink! You live in a box! Look at me! Look at the way I'm dressed! I made $500 last night and honey that didn't have anything to do with GOD!"

Old Ben showed no reaction as Katy spoke realizing that she was just putting on a brave face in the midst of great pain. Katy turned to look back down the street as the people began to file out of the church.

"Those people," she continued. "Those people in that church look at me and you like they stepped in something! That is if they bother to look at us at all! I went in there this morning and you know what happened? Nothing! The preacher preached about love and forgiveness, and everybody was huggin' on everybody but nobody hugged me! Oh no! They just stared at me like I was some kind of monster!"

Katy stood up again and walked in front of Old Ben as if trying to bring his attention to her outward appearance.

"I get more respect out here on the street than I got in that church!" Katy scoffed. "And as far as love is concerned, anybody that wants a piece of me is gonna have to pay for it!"

Old Ben looked up the street as he heard the sound of church bells and watched the people as they came out of the sanctuary. He then looked back to Katy and painfully said, "Somebody already did...Somebody paid the ultimate price for your love Kat and all He wants is for you to love Him back. It's not your choice to be out here like this. And the money is not making you happy. GOD wants to give you something that's gonna last.... Wouldn't you rather be with a GOD that can satisfy you for an eternity than to be with a man that can only satisfy you for a night? GOD don't care nothin' about what's on your outside Kat, He wants to get *in* you.... You have to learn to love yourself! As far as them church people go, I know what it feels like to be rejected and spit on, but those people ain't GOD. GOD IS LOVE!" Old Ben proclaimed excitedly. "That's what He's about, and if you ain't got love, you ain't got GOD! I know He's real whether I live in a mansion or live in a box. I can't explain Him but I know that He loves me. I know that He loves you too!"

Old Ben got up from the park bench and reached into the old shopping cart that he had with him and pulled out an old tattered bible and handed it to Katy. Katy reluctantly accepted the gift from Old Ben and he smiled. Without provocation he broke into a rousing chorus of *AMAZING GRACE* and tried to get Katy to join in. Katy flushed with embarrassment and looked around to see who was watching their encounter. When Katy turned back to face Old Ben he had made his way up the street still singing. His voice trailed off as he rounded the corner at the end of the block. Katy was introspective as she sat back down on the bench and intently studied the worn cover of the bible that Old Ben had given her.

"You don't need to be readin'," Sugar Man said from behind her as he snatched the bible from her hands and tossed it into a nearby trash bin. "You need to be workin'!"

Katy jumped up from the bench as Sugar Man tried to press his body against hers.

"I'm the only god you need," he teased. "And I ain't got nothin' but love for you baby!" he continued as he caressed her alabaster skin. "You can't afford to be turnin' down business either."

Katy tried to pull away from him but he grabbed her forcibly by the arm and hissed, "Read on your own time!"

Seeing two of the women from the church walking toward them Sugar Man made a show of his power over Katy. He grabbed her and kissed her passionately and she squirmed to pull free but he was too strong for her. The churchwomen that witnessed his mockery sighed in disgust and picked up the pace of their stride. After they passed Sugar Man let Katy go, strolled back to his car laughing, got in and drove away.

Katy spat vainly trying to eliminate the vile taste that he left in her mouth. She then wiped her mouth with the back of her hand and walked over to the trash bin where Sugar Man had discarded the bible. She retrieved the bible from the trash and gently wiped it off as if it were a precious family heirloom.

"They say you exist," she said looking up toward heaven. "And if you are real, I need you to be real for me, right here, right now!"

19

K.C. rolled over and lit a cigarette illuminating the dark room. He had one leg propped up on the bed and the other dangling off the side of it. A cool breeze blew in through the window causing his skin to tingle. He pulled the cover up over his leg and took a deep drag from his cigarette. He started to choke and he tried to muffle the sound of his cough so as not to disturb the nude figure lying next to him. Tears filled his eyes as he covered his mouth and wheezed. He put out his cigarette, jumped up from the bed, and went into the bathroom for water. He turned on the faucet, filled his cupped hands with water and took a drink. He then immersed his entire head into the water. He grabbed a towel from the rack over the toilet and dried his hair and face. The cooling effects of the water seemed to stabilize his attack. He stood naked in front of the mirror and stared at his reflection. With the exception of the cut through his left brow it was the same face. The same eyes, the same mouth, the same nose. K.C. stood before the mirror as if taking inventory of his body. As if he expected something to be wrong or different. "I'm okay," he whispered. A knock at the door gave him a start.

"K.C.!" shouted the man. "Are you all right in there?"

"Yeah! I'm all right!" K.C. sighed in relief. But as he continued to take inventory of his body he couldn't deny the most noticeable change in his appearance. K.C. had always been slight, but the amount of weight that he'd lost over the last several months made his bone structure more pronounced. "It's the crack," he whispered. K.C.'s brow furrowed as anxiety coursed through him. "It has to be the crack."

"KC!" the man called again. "Are you comin' out of there or do you want me to come in there after you?"

"I'll be out in a minute!" K.C. called back. "This isn't happenin'," K.C. thought to himself as he closed his eyes and leaned against the bathroom wall.

* * * * * * * * *

"The results of the viral load test are back," said the stone-faced doctor as he walked into the room. "Your T-cell count is lower than we expected. I think we should start an aggressive treatment for you right away. I also recommend that we check you into a drug rehab clinic so that we can begin to deal with your addiction."

K.C. sat on the side of the bed and recounted everything the doctor at the clinic said to him two weeks earlier, but he decided that the doctor was wrong. There was no way he could be HIV positive. He was tested right after Drake told him that he had AIDS. He had been extra careful with his partners. He never had unprotected sex. There was nothing wrong with him, he concluded. "I am not sick!"

"What did you say?" asked the man as he passed K.C. the crack pipe.

K.C. didn't answer. He stared for a long time at the paraphernalia in his hand in deep contemplation and then slowly put it to his lips and let the seduction of the smoke he inhaled work its magic. Before long he was no longer thinking about the doctor's prognosis. As far as he was concerned there was nothing to worry about. There was nothing wrong with him.

* * * * * * * * *

"Restoration is coming for you too!"

Old Ben's words continually infiltrated his dreams. K.C. woke up screaming. His body was wet with perspiration. His breathing was labored and his mind was in panic. He frantically scanned the room trying to remember where he was but the room was dark and he was unable to focus. A hand reached out and touched him in the darkness and he screamed again. He tangled himself up in the sheets as he tried to get out of bed and landed on the floor. "C'mere you little sissy!" It was his stepfather's voice. But it couldn't be, he was dead. K.C. scrambled trying to get up off the floor but the moisture on the bottom of his feet caused him to slip on the hard wood. He felt around in the dark like a blind man trying to find the light. "Help me!" he cried. "Somebody help me!"

Nobody heard K.C.'s cry for help, and the voices kept coming at him. Out of the abyss he could hear Elizabeth Goldberg saying, "Sovereign is who GOD is…You will get through this."

* * * * * * * * * *

The next morning Katy walked into K.C's room to find his naked body curled into the fetal position at the foot of his bed. His room looked as if a tornado had swept through it. His sheets were twisted on the floor, and his lamp was knocked over. Katy was immediately concerned for her friend's condition but did not want to alarm him by calling out his name. She sat down gently on his bed and softly touched her finger tips to his temple. K.C. cried out and jumped causing Katy to jump. Realizing that it was Katy he frantically grabbed her and held her tightly. Katy could feel K.C.'s heart pounding as if it was going to break out of his chest.

"K.C. what's wrong?" she pleaded.

"A nightmare," K.C. said in a whisper. "It was just a nightmare."

The sad reality was that K.C. had been diagnosed as HIV positive but he was bound and determined not to give voice to his fear. K.C. did not adjust his behavior according to what the doctor suggested. He continued to smoke marijuana and crack cocaine, he continued to have (safe) sex. However, his denial would cost him more than he could have imagined.

20

Kat and K.C. were sitting quietly together on the park bench taking in the afternoon sun when K.C. noticed two of the women from the church headed in their direction. Katy noticed them too and she reached down and pulled the tattered bible from her purse.

"I've been waiting for this!" Katy said gleefully.

As the women came closer Katy ran down to the sidewalk and started leafing through the bible. "Deuteronomy 10:19," she yelled causing the two women to stop. "Love ye therefore the stranger for ye were strangers in the land of Egypt!" The women assumed that Katy was ridiculing them so they kept walking but Katy would not let them pass. "Galatians 5:22, The fruit of the Spirit is love, joy, peace, long-suffering, gentleness, goodness, faith!" Katy continued becoming frustrated that the women would not listen. "1 John 4:7 Beloved, let us love one another for love is of God; and every one that loveth is born of God, and knoweth God...1 John 4:8 He that loveth not knoweth not God; for God is love!"

"Please!" the older of the two women sneered. "You don't know nothin' about the GOD I serve!"

"Amen, sistah! Amen!" the younger woman chimed in.

Seeing that together they were unable to push passed Katy, the two women separated and went around her. As they ran up the block toward the church rebuking Katy, she yelled one more scripture in her defense.

"1 John 4:11, Beloved, if God so loved us, we ought also to love one another!"

K.C. remained seated on the bench and watched in amazement as Katy went on her biblical tirade. He was so caught up in what she was doing that he didn't notice that Tee had crawled under the bench and gone through Katy's purse and took out several hundred dollars. Speed, who was passing by on his brand new bicycle, saw what Tee had done but he made no effort to speak up.

Flustered, Katy went back to the bench and sat next to K.C.
"What was that?"
"What was what?"
"That... GOD is love, and love is GOD, and love me, love me crap!"
"It's not crap, K.C.!" she said agitated. "Old Ben gave me this bible and I've been reading it and it's been helping me."
"Helpin' you what?" K.C. teased. "Lose your mind!"
"No," she said rubbing her hand across the bible's cover. "It's actually been helping me to find it. It's helped me find a lot of things."

K.C. heard the earnestness in Katy's tone so he began to take her more seriously. "What about this love thing?" he inquired.

"All my life," Katy began. "All I ever wanted was for somebody to love me. I never had anybody ever tell me that they loved *me*, not that I could believe anyway. Nobody except for my brother Kyle...K.C....all these men...this is nothing but sex. They don't love me and they don't love you either...not like you deserve to be loved."

"I love you Kat," he said as a coughing fit seized him. "You're all the family that I got. Besides as long as people like them label people like us, they ain't never gonna know who we are inside. When they look at me all they see is a "fag"."

"Stop it!" Katy demanded. "You know I hate that word. It just sounds so...dirty!"

Despite her objections K.C. continued to press his point. "FAG! HOMO! PUNK! SISSY! It don't matter, that's all they see, and when they look at you all they ever gonna see is a 'ho'! All you are to them is sin. They don't want us in their church can't you see that? They probably scared that we gonna rub off on 'em!"

As his anger intensified so did his coughing. "K.C... Are you all right?" Katy asked as she attempted to put her arm around him.

"I'm all right!" K.C. countered pushing her away. "I'm all right! I promise. I'll catch up with you later."

K.C. kissed Katy on the cheek and headed up the street. As he disappeared from sight Katy's sun was blocked by Sugar Man's shadow. He had come to collect the money that Tee had just stolen from her. When Katy leaned over to pick up her purse, she discovered that the money was gone. She panicked as she tried to come up with a plausible explanation. Sugar Man went ballistic as Katy attempted to retrace her steps. She told him that she knew she'd had the money when she and K.C. had come to sit in the park. Her mind immediately conjured up images of K.C., her trusted friend, taking the money from her to go and buy drugs. But her heart warred against that possibility. Sugar Man was furious and would not be placated by her excuses. He grabbed Katy's purse and dumped its contents on the ground.

"I'll tell you what we're gonna do...We're gonna go find that punk K.C.," Sugar Man seethed as he pulled Katy from the bench by her hair. His nostrils flared with anger and Katy saw the look in his eyes. The look that he had when he attacked her father in her dorm room. The look that he had when he argued with Cookie in the club. The look he had when he had thrown her across the hotel room floor when she had attacked him. It was that look that frightened her. "If K.C. has my money," Sugar Man continued. "I'm gonna beat it out of him! And if we don't find him...I'm gonna enjoy beating it out of you!"

Sugar Man dragged Katy from the park kicking and screaming and shoved her into his car. None of the passersby dared to interfere assuming that it was just a lover's quarrel and justice would be better served if they tended to their own business.

As Sugar Man's red Mercedes tore up the road, Old Ben was making his way through the trail in the park singing *AMAZING GRACE* and enjoying the beautiful spring whether. As he got closer to the bench where Katy had been he noticed her purse laying on the ground and the old tattered bible beside it. He was heartsick as he took it to mean that Katy had a date with disaster. He knelt down slowly and picked up the contents of her purse and put everything back inside. He then picked up the sullied bible as tears filled his eyes. He buried his face in its torn pages and wept.

* * * * * * * * * *

Sugar Man and Katy looked in every conceivable place that K.C. could have gone, but they didn't find him. At every stop Sugar Man's anger intensified but not so much because of the loss of the money, but because he assumed that Katy and K.C. had plotted to scam him and he wasn't about to be had. Sugar Man was not the sort of man that took loss of any kind well, and he wasn't going to let them think they had gotten one over on him.

Katy sat nervously in the passenger seat of the car biting her bottom lip. "Why would K.C. take money from her?" she thought trying to figure out his motives. She glanced out of the corner of her eye and saw Sugar Man silently fuming. His jawbone tensed and she could almost swear that his knuckles were turning white from gripping the steering wheel so tightly.

"There he is!" Sugar Man exclaimed as he accelerated and crossed three lanes of traffic, causing an accident. It turned out that his eyesight needed as much help as his driving. The man that he spotted was not K.C. Sugar Man spouted several colorful expletives and sped away from the scene of the accident that he'd caused.

Daylight was giving way to dusk. Having exhausted every possible place that K.C. could be, Katy thought that Sugar Man was finally taking her back to her apartment. However, as he got closer to her street he took a turn that led off in the opposite direction.

"Where are we going now?" Katy asked nervously.

Sugar Man didn't answer, instead he kept his eyes fixed in front of him and continued on course. He stopped the car at a dead end on the far south side of town.

Katy looked around as a horrible feeling of anxiety fell over her. "Please don't tell me that you want me to do a *john* out here."

Before she knew what was happening the back of Sugar Man's hand smacked her across her face and in rapid succession he hit her in the nose. He then immediately grabbed her by the throat and pulled her to him so that they were eye to eye. The sting of his hand caused her eyes to tear up and a trickle of blood ran out of her nose. She attempted to loosen his hold around her neck but the more she tried the more pressure he applied. Katy gasped for every breath as Sugar Man began to speak.

"I don't know what kind of a fool you take me for," he said in a low menacing whisper. "But I am not going to be taken advantage of by you and that punk K.C.... Do I make myself clear?"

Katy nodded in response as she felt the air passage closing in her throat.

"You have messed with the wrong man little girl. I *will* kill you! I can be your best friend, or I can be your worst nightmare. It's up to you to decide how you want to play the game, but make no mistake... *I* will not lose. You will not leave me until I want you too, understand?"

Katy nodded again as her eyes closed. She wanted to let go. She wanted him to kill her. She wanted her freedom. At the precise moment that life was about to leave her body, Sugar Man released his grip. Katy's body went limp. He gently cupped her face in his hands and wiped the blood away with his finger.

"You see," he said as he licked the blood from his finger. "We're connected. No matter how you try to deny it, you will always be drawn to me."

With a smattering of blood on his lips he gently kissed Katy and let her slump like a sack of potatoes against the door as he started up the car and drove off.

* * * * * * * * * *

"Get some sleep," he said as Katy got out of his car in front of her building. "Earl's got somebody he wants you to meet tomorrow."

Katy closed her eyes and swallowed hard to suppress the feeling of nausea that welled up inside her. Every fiber of her being filled with loathing for Sugar Man as she slowly ascended the stairs to her apartment. It wasn't until she got to the door that she realized that she didn't have her keys. "My purse!" she sighed. She stood at the door and searched her mind trying to remember where she left it. She made her way back down the stairs and across the street to the park. As she approached the bench where she sat earlier she could see the shadowy figure of a man seated on the bench. "B..Ben," she stammered. Old Ben didn't say anything he just looked at her with eyes full of compassion and gave her back the bible and her purse. "Thank you," Katy said softly. As she turned to walk away she threw the bible in the trashcan. "I won't be needing this anymore!"

"Jesus said," Old Ben began. "I am the door. If anyone enters by Me, he will be saved, and will go in and out and find pasture. The thief does not come except to steal, and to kill, and to destroy. I have come that you may have life, and that you may have it more abundantly ... Restoration means the replacing of spiritual *death* with spiritual *life!*"

"I don't want to hear anymore!" Katy pleaded without turning back to face him. "Leave me alone! Just leave me alone!" Katy found it hard to look at Old Ben for very long. His eyes spoke volumes to her pain. Whenever she looked at him she sensed that he could see straight through to her soul and it confused her. What troubled her more was the feeling that she didn't know how to put words to the way he made her feel. He knew her somehow but she never knew how or on what level.

"Sugar Man is killing you," Old Ben said gravely.

"He's all I've got!" Katy cried.

"You don't believe that!" Old Ben insisted. "Call your Father," he implored.

"My father doesn't want to have anything to do with me," Katy lamented.

"I wasn't talkin' about that father," Old Ben responded.

Katy arduously turned and looked at Old Ben and saw that he was crying too. She walked over to the trashcan and reverently removed the bible.

"It's not too late," Old Ben admonished as he placed his leathery old hand on top of hers but Katy didn't feel the roughness of his skin, she only felt his gentleness.

There were a lot of homeless indigents in and around the neighborhood but none that were as autonomous as Old Ben. There was Gussie "the crazy bag lady", who talked to herself and ate out of garbage cans. And Jim who claims to have lost both his legs in the war, though every time he told the story it was a different war. Jim hung out down at the train station with a guitar and a can for which he solicited spare change from passersby. Katy always made it a point to give him a couple of dollars even if he couldn't remember how he lost his legs. Then there was Hank, Al, and Walt who frequented the park area sleeping under trees or in doorways of buildings when the weather dictated. The three of them found their comfort and strength in sharing the mellifluous contents of a brown paper bag. To society at large they were considered the nameless, faceless, exiled denizens of crime and intemperance but as Katy found out, much like herself, most of them were just the victims of circumstance. But Old Ben was different. Sometimes what he had to say could frighten her and at other times, like now, without saying much at all he gave her an overwhelming sense of hope.

Katy offered Old Ben a wry smile and ran back through the park to her apartment building. Rosetta, who had just come from midweek service at the church, was crossing at the corner with her grandchildren. Byron, who she held in her arms, threw his ball out into the street, and Brandy let go of Rosetta's hand and ran after it.

"Brandy!" Rosetta screamed in horror as she saw a car careening around the corner toward Brandy. As Katy approached the corner she saw that the car showed no signs of slowing down. She took off in a dead run and snatched Brandy out of the street. With Brandy safely locked in her arms the two ducked and rolled into a row of parked cars. The commotion brought the residents of the building to their windows and doors and brought those in the park, who were close enough to hear, to the edge of a bank of trees, including Old Ben.

"Are you okay?" Katy asked as she caught her breath.

Brandy was visibly shaken but with the exception of skinned knees and elbows she wasn't hurt. Katy, oblivious to her own bruises, removed a tissue from her purse and spat on it to wipe the blood from Brandy's knee.

"Get your hands off my grand baby!" Rosetta shrieked.

"She's all right," Katy offered. "She's just a little shaken up."

"Brandy are you okay?" Rosetta asked sternly.

Brandy nodded her head and stood to her feet. Rosetta took her by the hand and started to pull her away as a crowd of people started to gather around Katy.

"You people!" Rosetta huffed as she walked away. "No tellin' what kind of nasty germs you have given my grand baby. Now I got to take her to the hospital!"

As a couple of guys helped Katy to her feet Brandy stopped Rosetta's harangue and ran back toward Katy much to Rosetta's disdain.

"Thank you for savin' me," Brandy said softly, then she turned back and ran to her grandmother. Rosetta continued to fuss at Brandy for having been so careless as they walked on. Katy brushed herself off and went into her building.

Her encounter with Brandy prompted Katy to try and call her father. As she attended to her cuts and bruises she wondered what she would say to him after all this time. She hesitantly picked up the phone and dialed but she hung up before she completed the call. To calm herself she lit a cigarette and poured a shot of gin. Once her jangled nerves were settled she dialed the number again.

"Hello," came the voice of the new Mrs. Jennings.

Katy's throat went dry and she almost slammed the receiver down but she took a deep breath and pressed on.

"I'd like to speak to my father," Katy said coolly.

"Who may I ask is calling?" responded the acrimonious female.

Katy resisted the urge to dispense a verbal bashing and continued on. "This is his daughter."

"His daughter?" she sneered.

"Look!" Katy snapped. "Will you please put my father on the phone!"

"I'm afraid that's impossible," gibed the shrewish woman. "My husband is out of town."

Defeated, Katy was just about to hang up the phone when she heard the woman call her by name.

"Katy... We received a letter from Northwestern. Kyle knows that you've dropped out and he's very, very angry with you. He thinks you've gotten yourself all mixed up with some black man. Please tell me he's exaggerating. Tell me you're not that asinine."

No longer able to resist the urge, Katy attacked the woman with a barrage of stinging expletives and slammed down the phone.

21

Family curses can be passed on in much the same way as eye color, hair color, and personality traits. Generational curses. The ancestor of sin is sin. If sin is not dealt with in one generation it will rear its ugly head in another. Have you ever looked at a child and said, "He looks just like grandfather used to when he was that age." Or, "She acts just like her mother." Have you noticed that the good gets passed along with the bad?

Numbers 14:18 The LORD is longsuffering, and of great mercy, forgiving iniquity and transgression, and by no means clearing the guilty, visiting the iniquity of the fathers upon the children unto the third and fourth generation.

* * * * * * * * *

There had never been a time in her life that Rosetta ever wanted to revisit the shame and degradation that she fought to arrest from her past. Rosetta became pregnant for the first time when she was 15 years old. The eldest daughter of a staunch southern Baptist preacher left to fend for herself and take care of her four younger siblings after her mother died in childbirth. Not a year had passed before her father took another wife who had three children of her own.

It wasn't something she was proud of but she was attracted to her 17-year-old stepbrother and he also found it hard to resist being attracted to her. One late afternoon in the heat of the Alabama sun their passions got the best of them and Jerome was conceived. Rosetta's father nearly beat his stepson to death and he banished his pregnant daughter to live with her maternal grandmother Thelma in Kentucky. Rosetta barely saw her family again after that. The strain of what happened between Rosetta and her stepbrother James took its toll on the entire family, it even caused her father and his new wife to separate and eventually divorce. Saddled with the burden of what she'd done to her family Rosetta tried to forget James and put the whole sordid mess behind her but she couldn't. She tried to contact James several times but he wanted nothing to do with her or the baby that she chose to keep. Three years after moving to Kentucky her grandmother died leaving her alone with a small baby to take care of. Rosetta sought comfort in the arms of a handsome young soldier home on leave. Four weeks after he shipped out to Ft. Bragg in Fayetteville, North Carolina, Rosetta found herself pregnant again, this time with Tee. She never heard from her young soldier again.

With nowhere else to go Rosetta took a job as a clerk in a local department store to support herself and her children. The money wasn't great but the company did offer benefits and that was the best thing for her, she thought, in the absence of a husband. Fortunately she didn't have to worry about a place to live. Her grandmother left her the house after she died, at least what there was of it. Rosetta often thought about selling it but she knew that she wouldn't get much for it in its condition so she stayed and made the best of it.

By the time she turned 25 Rosetta had worked her way up to department manager. She had even been dating for the better part of a year. On the surface Sam Burnette appeared to be the perfect mate for her, there had even been talk of marriage. However, Sam had a secret that would have made marriage to Rosetta impossible, he was already married. Technically he was separated but Rosetta was not about to allow herself to become his mistress. When she found out he was married she thought that she could wait it out but a divorce was not forthcoming.

Rosetta applied for a job transfer to a sister store in Chicago and sold her grandmother's house for what she could get for it. Along with her 10 year old son Jerome and seven year old Thelma (Tee), she left the countryside of Kentucky for the urban streets of the windy city.

As she stood in the moonlit window of her bedroom looking out over the community she had settled in, Rosetta lamented that this was not the same neighborhood it once was. Even though it had never been the posh upscale vicinity in and around Lakeshore Drive it wasn't rampant with crime. Drugs and prostitution were not shoved down your throat with the morning coffee. She was certain that the environment contributed to the downfall of her children and now she had her grandchildren to raise but how was she supposed to do that any differently than she had raised Jerome and Tee. How was she supposed to protect them from the onslaught of a decaying society? "GOD help me," she moaned as tears welled in her eyes.

Rosetta stood in the window for hours in introspection. She maligned and berated the woman she had become, the fact that she had never married, the kind of children she raised, and the kind of mother she had been to them. She hated herself for her choices, her mistakes, and the state she found herself in. She stood in the window oblivious to time. Watching the freak show that played out underneath her bedroom window as she thought that her daughter was out there among the fray. Tee was out there somewhere in the dark paying for the sins of another, and reaping the reproach of her own.

22

K.C. quietly turned the key in the door to the apartment that he shared with Katy. It was almost noon the next day and he had been out all night. The light from the hallway flooded into the room before him and eerily lit the shadowy figure that sat in wait for him.

"Where have you been all night?" Katy demanded.

"Kat you scared me," K.C. said as he clutched his chest and caught his breath.

Katy had waited to confront K.C. all night concerning Sugar Man's stolen money. The money that she had adulterated her body for. The money that Sugar Man was willing to kill her for. Bitterness had eaten at her all night. Even though she hadn't wanted to, the thought that K.C. had stolen the money became more fact to her than fiction.

"Oh my God what happened to you?" K.C. inquired as he saw the bruises on Katy's arms and face. He closed the door and turned on the light in the room to get a better look. Assuming the worst he approached Katy and reached out to her, she withdrew from him and jumped up from the sofa.

"Who did this to you?" he continued. "Was it one of your *johns*? Was it Sugar Man? Kat talk to me…Who did this?"

"You did!" Katy shrieked as she turned to look at him.

"Me!" K.C. said in amazement at the striking accusation. "Girl are you high or somethin'?"

"You did this!" she repeated.

"You're crazy!" K.C. shouted defensively. "I don't know what you're talkin' about!"

"You took $600 of Sugar Man's money out of my purse!"

Katy said as she opened up her purse to him as if to show him the violation.

"That's crazy!" K.C. said in disbelief. "I would never steal from you! You know that!"

Katy threw her purse across the room folded her arms in distress and stared out the window. "All I know is that you were with me yesterday when I had the money and when you left the money was gone too!"

Fuming over the fact that this girl that he had come to know as family stood there accusing him of such a horrible thing K.C. began to pace back and forth trying to make sense out of what could have happened.

"I ... I ... I can't believe this," he stuttered. "Why would I steal from you! Why! You and me, we're family. I wouldn't do that to you, you know that!"

Katy turned away from the window and looked at him pleadingly. "K.C. tell me the truth...please."

"I AM TELLIN' YOU THE TRUTH!!!" he screamed. "Why would I steal from you?"

"So you can buy crack and reefer that's why!" Katy retorted. "I don't know maybe you had a slow day yesterday and nobody wanted to buy what you were selling!"

Wounded was the only way to describe how K.C. looked at Katy in the wake of her biting insinuation.

"That was low Kat...even for you."

Frustrated, angry, and confused Katy grabbed her jacket and ran out of the apartment. Realizing that she might do something even more self destructive K.C. ran after her. As Katy reached the street Speed ran out in front of her nearly knocking her down, but Old Ben, who happened to be coming up the opposite end of the sidewalk grabbed Speed and stopped him.

"Whoa!" Old Ben chided Speed. "Where are you off to in such a hurry?"

"Get yo' filthy hands off me old man before I cut yo' heart out!" Speed yelled as he tried to squirm free of Old Ben. "Let go of me man! Let go!"

Old Ben held fast to Speed and dragged him back over to where Katy and K.C. were standing.

"Tell her," Old Ben said firmly to Speed. "Go on tell her!"

"I ain't tellin' her nothin'!" Speed insisted as he continued to struggle.

Old Ben grabbed Speed's face and forced him to look at Katy. "Look at her!" he demanded. "Look at what that low life hustler did to her! You tell her what she needs to know and you tell her right now!"

It dawned on K.C. that Speed had something to do with the money disappearing so he yanked Speed from Old Ben's clutches and held him high up off the ground letting his legs dangle in the air.

"You little punk!" K.C. started. "Do you know somethin' about what happened to Kat's money? Did you take it?"

Speed was fearless. He would not let K.C. intimidate him. "I didn't take nothin'! That old man don't know *jack* about nothin'!"

K.C.'s anger was seething and he wanted to end this '*witch hunt*'. "If you know somethin' you better tell her right now or I will break your scrawny little neck!" K.C. viciously shook Speed and Katy tried to intercede. "You don't believe me punk! I killed somebody once before, don't make me do it again!"

"It was Tee!" Speed shouted. "She took the money! I saw her! She took it and ran off with it!"

Convinced that Speed had told the truth, K.C. threw him to the ground. Speed jumped up and ran off. When he got to the end of the block Speed turned back around and flashed K.C. '*the bird*' and disappeared around the corner.

"Now do you believe me?" K.C. asked Katy as he turned and walked away.

Katy ran after K.C. and grabbed him by the arm. "K.C. I'm...I'm sorry." '*Sorry*' was such a sorry word to use as an apology for the verbal abuse that she had inflicted upon K.C. She sadly watched her friend walk away and wondered if she had caused irreparable damage to the only relationship that had meant anything to her since her brother Kyle. "How could I have accused him? How could I have believed that he could have done something so horrible as to deliberately hurt me?"

* * * * * * * * *

K.C. walked until he found himself at a pool hall six blocks away from his apartment. The entire time all he thought about was Katy's accusations. He thought she trusted him. He thought she cared about him. He thought they were family. But now he felt that there was no one he could trust but himself. There was no one he could depend on. It was early in the day and the pool hall was virtually empty and dimly lit. K.C. sat alone in a dark corner of the room staring into a glass of beer. His mind was a montage of images and thoughts. He thought about his mother, he thought about Drake, he thought about the thing that he'd become. All the men that he had been with, both for profit and pleasure, all the drugs, all the parties, all the sadness. Oddly he thought about Elizabeth Goldberg the unobtrusive stranger that journeyed along with him as he began his maniacal odyssey into nowhere over seven years ago. "You will get through this," he whispered to himself as he downed the glass of beer. As K.C. started to get up from the booth and go to the bar for another glass his attention was drawn to the voice he heard talking on the pay phone on the other side of the partition.

"Yeah, it's me…I didn't want to take the chance of callin' you on the cell phone."

K.C. heard the unmistakable drawl of Sugar Man and he listened intently as the conversation continued.

"Did my stuff come in? How many kilos? No I don't want to wait! Let's do it now! No not there that place is gettin' too hot. Meet me down at that place on Indiana Avenue in about an hour…Yeah that's the place. Don't double cross me Milo you know what will happen to you if you do!"

When K.C. heard Sugar Man hang up he slumped in his seat and pulled his cap down over his face. He heard footsteps approaching the table where he was and got a little anxious thinking that it was Sugar Man.

"You want another beer? Asked the grouse proprietor of the pool hall. K.C. didn't acknowledge the man verbally he shook his head and waved the man away. As the proprietor turned to go K.C. nervously peeked out from under his cap in time to see Sugar Man exiting. He breathed a sigh of relief as he sat up and pulled off his cap. Suddenly, as if someone had turned on a light inside his head, a wicked smile formed on K.C.'s lips and his eyes lit up. Overhearing Sugar Man's conversation he realized that he was privy to information that would get this menace off the street and away from Katy. K.C. got up from the table, went over to the payphone and dialed '0'. His entire countenance changed as he said gleefully, "Operator get me the police!"

* * * * * * * * *

The news that Sugar Man was busted while making a drug deal spread through the community like wild fire. Chicago's finest had not only captured Sugar Man and several of his associates; they also took a sizable bite out of his bank account to the tune of $500,000. When Katy discovered that Sugar Man had been arrested she was ecstatic. As she sat in her room watching the televised report of his arrest she laughed out loud, for the first time in what seemed like ages, she laughed out loud.

"It feels good doesn't it?" K.C. asked leaning against the door of her room.

Katy jumped in surprise and stared sorrowfully at her friend.

"I guess he won't be botherin' you any more," K.C. smiled.

"K.C..." Katy started as she turned off the television and got up from her bed. "Please forgive me. I'm so sorry that I accused you of stealing that money."

Without saying a word K.C. walked into the bedroom toward Katy and held out his arms to her. How childlike and innocent she looked standing there in the center of the room trembling. Much like the old Katy in a pair of comfortable jeans and a baggy sweatshirt. The same sweatshirt that K.C. had given her months before. K.C. lovingly took Katy in his arms and held her tightly.

"I know you're scared," he whispered. "I'm scared too, but we will get through this."

Katy buried her face into the hollow of K.C.'s arms and sobbed uncontrollably. K.C. stood strong and protective but he could not resist the urge to cry himself. One single solitary tear trickled down his face but it alone held the agony of his heart.

* * * * * * * * *

Over a week had passed since Sugar Man's arrest and the neighborhood seemed all the better for it. Katy woke up to the sound of the birds singing and the sun beaming brightly through her bedroom window. She went to the kitchen to fix breakfast and realized that they were out of eggs, there was no milk either, and the only bread left was moldy and green. Katy dressed quickly and grabbed her purse to go to the store.

"$4.75," she sighed as she counted the pittance she found. She sat down on the sofa, threw her head back, and ran her slender fingers through her shoulder length blonde hair. "$4.75," she said again in disgust.

"Hey," K.C. muttered as he emerged from his bedroom in a coughing fit. "Are you O.K.?"

"Yeah I'm fine," Katy responded. "Are you O.K.?"

"Peachy!" K.C. said between coughs. "Just peachy!"

As he went into the bathroom Katy became more than a little alarmed at the severity of his coughing spell. She was also concerned that his body seemed drawn and sickly in appearance. Katy assumed that the change in K.C. was because of his increased crack use. She had encouraged him more than once over the last several weeks to go to the clinic, but he was totally against her suggestion. Katy continued to sit on the sofa as the breeze of the warm spring air brushed over her. Instinctively she picked up the phone, just to check, but it was still disconnected and had been for a couple of days. Rent was due the next week, there was no food in the house and she had $4.75 to her name. "I need a real job," Katy thought to herself as the bathroom door opened and K.C. came out.

"What's the matter?" he asked.

"Are you all right K.C.?"

"Yes! I'm O.K... now get off my back!"

K.C. went back to his room and slammed the door behind him. His behavior was confusing and their living situation wasn't helping. She felt she had to so something to bring money into the house. She was willing to do anything except hit the streets. Katy grabbed her purse and left the apartment.

She ended up down at Gemini's asking Otis for work. He informed her that there wasn't anything available there and referred her to several other places. She didn't have any luck anywhere else either. As the day wore on and the possibilities for employment waned Katy ended up walking into a McDonald's and asking for an application.

"I know you can do better than that!"

Katy turned and saw Cookie standing behind her. Embarrassed Katy tried to hide the application behind her back.

"Please tell me that that application is not for you."

"Cookie what are you doing here?" Katy nervously asked.

"I like the fries," Cookie responded as she stepped passed Katy and up to the register to order. "You want somethin'?" she asked turning back to Katy.

"No...No thank you," Katy responded apprehensively as the line behind her continued to form.

Ignoring her Cookie turned back to the cashier and ordered for the two of them. Katy sheepishly found a table and quietly sat down. Dressed as provocatively as she was Cookie solicited a lot of attention from the men, as well as the women, but she didn't care.

"After you eat your hamburger," she whispered seductively to a man behind her, "if you want a little chocolate chip for dessert... I'll be sittin' over there."

With that she picked up her tray of food and joined Katy.

"O.K. girl what's goin' on?" Cookie asked opening her eyes after blessing her food.

"You pray?" Katy scoffed.

"Yeah...So!" Cookie retorted. "What of it!"

"It's just that..." Katy responded more seriously.

"... 'ho's can't pray is that it!" Cookie interrupted.

Katy looked away from Cookie without answering.

"Eat your fries before they get cold," Cookie continued. Katy hesitantly picked up the box and slowly started to eat. "O.K. now what's goin' on with you and K.C.? Why is the phone disconnected? Why are you fillin' out job applications to work at McDonald's? Just because Sugar is locked up don't mean you can't work."

"I don't want that kind of work!" Katy sniped.

Cookie took a deep breath as she flashed back on the night she saw Sugar Man slip the *roofies* into Katy's drink. "Look...Kat," she began. "It may not be the job of choice, but it's a job. You'll make more money out there on the street in one day than you could workin' in a place like this for a whole week. Besides if you really want out now is the perfect time."

Katy looked at Cookie in astonishment at the concern in her voice.

"Don't look at me like that," Cookie chided as she took a sip of her drink. "All I mean is that with Sugar locked up if you want to get out of Chicago now would be the perfect time to get out. But you ain't goin' no where without money."

Katy hated to admit it but Cookie was right. She may not have wanted to do it but in order to make the kind of money she needed she had to *go to work* for it.

"When you pray," Katy asked tentatively. "Do you pray to GOD?"

"Who did you think I was prayin' to... *Sugar Man*?

Katy looked puzzled, which let Cookie know that she was clueless. After a few minutes she pressed on. "If you pray to GOD, does that mean you believe He exists?"

"I asked a blessing over my food!" Cookie responded sharply. "It's not a crime!"

"Is that the only praying you ever do?" Katy continued. "Blessing your food I mean."

"What is this 20 questions?" Cookie snapped. "Look its just somethin' you do all right! I've always done it ever since I was a little girl."

Katy could see that her questions were making Cookie uncomfortable so she decided to back off. Cookie got up from the table, grabbed the tray and threw her half-eaten French fries in the trash.

"Sugar Man's not gonna be locked up forever," she said as she put on her sunglasses. "When he gets out, and don't fool yourself he will get out, he's gonna be mad as the devil. If you're gonna go I suggest you get a move on!"

Katy continued to sit at the table for a long time after Cookie left. She stared at her reflection in the window for what seemed an eternity before she too got up and walked out. As she headed up the street toward the bus stop a man driving a dark blue sedan pulled up along side her.

"Where ya' headed?" he asked as he rolled down his tinted window.

Katy ignored him and picked up her pace. Undaunted, the car continued following her and the man continued talking. As he talked Katy considered Cookie's advice in the restaurant. She stopped, looked around, and walked over to the car.

"I live on the West Side," she said as she leaned in the window.

"Hop in!" the man responded leering at Katy lustfully.

When Katy got into the car the man took his hand and ran it up her leg and under her skirt. Katy winced and pulled away as she heard Cookie's voice in her head, "...with Sugar locked up if you want to get out of Chicago now would be the perfect time to get out. But you ain't goin' no where without money." Hearing those words again Katy closed her eyes, relaxed, and allowed the man to fondle her.

* * * * * * * * *

When Katy left the motel room she felt more repulsed than when she was forced to do Sugar Man's bidding. She tried to convince herself that this was a means to an end, but it turned her stomach as she wondered to what end. She would never be able to talk about the things that went on inside that room. When she was picked up she assumed that it would just be "straight sex" with the odd looking man in the horn-rimmed glasses, how could she have known that he wanted her to participate in "group activities." As revolting as Earl had been she had not felt the total abhorrence that she felt inside that motel room. She pulled at her clothes as she walked swiftly up the street and away from the motel. She tried to hail a taxi but none would stop, so she kept walking. She started to cry as she caught her reflection in the window of a corner market. She was a mess. She was in such a hurry to get out of the motel room that she hadn't bothered to fix herself up. Her hair was a mess, her blouse was on the wrong side, and her mascara had run giving her a ghoulish appearance. She stood looking at herself trying to fix her hair and wipe the remains of the makeup from her face.

"I was trying to help you before you fell in. Now it's my job to help you get out."

It was Old Ben's voice seemingly calling to her out of the evening breeze. She turned around sharply but he wasn't there.

"Ben!" Katy called out. "Ben are you there? Ben I need help. Please help me."

It was 10 p.m. by the clock she saw through the window of the little market. She was in an unfamiliar part of town. Most of the buildings on the street were deserted and boarded up. The street was littered with abandoned cars with broken windows or missing tires. Katy was petrified as she walked back in the direction that she had come. The only sound she could hear was the sound of her heart pounding in her ears. Her eyes widened as the intensity of her walk became a run. The heels on her shoes clicked fiercely on the pavement and echoed through the darkness. Just as she rounded the corner at the end of the block a man stepped out of the shadows. A blood-curdling scream erupted from deep inside of her as she backed up and ran back in the other direction. The itinerant stranger gave chase and eventually trapped her at the end of the dead end street. "No!" Katy screamed as she realized that there was no escape. Undaunted the man stopped running and continued to move menacingly toward her rubbing the back of his hand across his mouth. He was dirty and the hair was matted on his head and face. When he got close enough for her to see his face and feel his breath on her skin a police siren rang out from the end of the block, and the man scurried through a hole at the bottom of a chain link fence and disappeared.

"Help me! Help me!" Katy screamed as she ran to the police car waving her arms frantically.

"Are you all right?" the officer inquired as he got out of his cruiser and moved toward her.

Katy fell into his arms clinging to him as if he were a life preserver. Her breathing was so erratic she couldn't answer. The officer helped her into his cruiser as he asked her again if she was all right. Katy nodded an affirmative response. "Where do you live?" he continued. It took a moment for Katy to catch her breath enough to answer. The officer was all too familiar with the address that she'd given him. "Do you want to file a report?" asked the officer. "Are you hurt? Do you need to go to the hospital?"

"No! I'm not hurt!" Katy cried. "I don't want to file a report and I don't want to go to the hospital…Please…please I just want to go home…Please!"

Although she was shaken up the officer could see that she wasn't physically hurt. Ordinarily he should have called into the station, however since he was off duty he decided that he would escort Katy home.

"This is no kind of life for you, you know that don't you?" he asked as he looked at her through his rear view mirror. "That man could have raped you even worse he could have killed you."

Katy nodded her head as she nervously removed a cigarette from her purse.

"You can't smoke in here," continued the officer.

Katy smirked and put the cigarette back in her purse. While they drove through the streets Katy listened to the police radio announcing one violent crime after the other.

"That could have been you tonight," the officer said sternly. "It was just the grace of GOD that saved you."

A lump formed in Katy's throat as she took a closer look at the officer. The words to the song she'd heard in the church came back to her. *Amazing grace how sweet the sound that saved a wretch like me. I once was lost but now I'm found, was blind but now I see.*

When the policeman dropped her off he gave her a flyer to his church. "You should come sometime," he said. "You'll never be the same again, I can promise you that."

Katy thanked the officer again and he drove off after she assured him that she would be all right. She stood on the sidewalk and stared at the flyer in her hand. Suddenly she crossed the street to the park in search of Old Ben. She found him sleeping on the park bench and turned to walk away.

"You came lookin' for me," he said raising his head off the rumpled coat he was using as a pillow. "Don't walk away now that you've found me."

He sat up and despite herself Katy drew closer to him. "How can you help me get out?" Katy asked staring him squarely in the eye. "You don't have anything! You have less than me! You're sleeping on a park bench! How can you help me? Why do I see your face or hear your voice everywhere I go? Why are you haunting me?"

Old Ben returned Katy's stare and stood up to address her. "You're not haunted by me," he said quietly. "You're haunted by guilt…. What's that in your hand?"

"Nothing," Katy said as she crumpled up the flyer and threw it in the trash. "Just a piece of paper."

"When are going to stop letting men ball you up and throw you away like you just did that paper?" Old Ben asked as he slowly sat back down on the bench. "Kat you know what love is, and *this* ain't it. You read it for yourself. GOD loves you."

"Yeah?" Katy sniped. "Then why don't I feel GOD's love, huh? Why is pain the only thing I feel?

"Because you won't let yourself be loved. You feel that you don't have the right to be loved. You weren't responsible for your brother's death or your mother's."

Katy's mouth dropped open and she looked at him astounded that he would know about Kyle or her mother. "Who are you?" she asked hesitantly.

Old Ben ignored her question and continued to press his point. "You want to blame yourself for things you had no control over and when you couldn't make your father pay, you decided to pay by letting go of your self-respect, your dignity, and your future."

Katy's eyes began to cloud and she felt an unexplainable burning in the pit of her stomach.

"Why did you call me tonight?" Old Ben continued. "Why did you come looking for me?"

Katy couldn't answer she just stood there as tears streamed down her face. She felt naked in front of him. All her pretense, all her bravado, all her hostility was stripped away.

"Kat, no one can love you enough to get rid of that kind of pain. The only one that can love you that much is GOD and His love is unconditional.... Do you believe in GOD?" Old Ben asked. Katy closed her eyes to keep from looking at him but she couldn't move. "Do you believe in GOD?" he repeated.

Katy reflected on the endless string of men that she allowed to debase her over the months. She reflected on the man that had picked her up earlier and the unspeakable things that he and his cohorts had done to her inside the motel room. She reflected on the vagrant that chased her down in the street afterwards. She reflected on the words of GOD's grace that the police officer had spoken as he drove her home. Katy stood trembling and crying before Old Ben as her resolve melted away.

"Yes," she whimpered. "Yes I believe in GOD."

Seeing that Katy was on the verge of surrender Old Ben stood up and went to her. "Do you believe that GOD is the only one that can save you now! He died so that you can live! He *wants* you to live! You may not see it now but if you would only believe it that's the first step. All you have to do is believe!...

Jesus said, *"My grace is sufficient for you, for My strength is made perfect in your weakness."*

GRACE. Unmerited favor. Divine love and protection given to mankind by GOD.

"I'm so tired of hurting." Katy anguished. "I'm just so tired."

Katy collapsed in Old Ben's arms and together they fell on their knees.

"Take the first step Kat," Old Ben admonished. "GOD is waiting for you. He's waiting to take the pain away. He's waiting to give you the love that you've always wanted. *Watch* to *see* what He will say. GOD is a GOD of action. He doesn't do a whole lot of unnecessary talking, but when He talks, He does what He says He's going to do. All you have to do is believe…Say it…Say it Kat!"

There was no more fight left in her, no more resistance, no more holding back.

"I believe," Katy cried. "Yes…I believe."

23

K.C. sat straight up in his bed as an overwhelming sensation of nausea swept over him. The drugs that he'd been prescribed were doing a number on his system and the side effects were making him feel worse. Besides the nausea there was the diarrhea, night sweats, and numbness that he sometimes felt in his arms and legs, not to mention the weight loss. He barely managed to get up and put on his clothes yet he still couldn't tell Katy that something was wrong, he couldn't tell anybody, he was hardly able to admit it to himself. K.C. laid back on the wall to support his head and stared out his bedroom window. Life was going on as usual. People were on their way to work. Children were on their way to school. Traffic was backed up all over the city. And there he stood in the window watching, all he could do anymore was watch.

He picked up the phone to call Cookie but he remembered that the phone was disconnected. So he decided, after staying in the house all day the day before, that he would venture out and walk to her place. He grabbed his jacket so that he could cover himself and he also donned a cap and sunglasses, so as not to draw attention to the noticeable changes. When he opened his bedroom door he could smell bacon frying.

"Good morning!" Katy said pleasantly smiling at him.

Even though her encounter in the motel the night before had been a nightmare she made enough money to buy some food and pay the rent. But that was not the reason she smiled. The reason she smiled was because of her encounter with GOD. Katy felt a freedom and a peace that she had not known in her life.

"I hope you're hungry," she said pouring orange juice into two glasses.

K.C. didn't have an appetite but he saw the trouble she had gone to so he sat down at the table to eat. He could tell right away that there was something different about his friend but he couldn't put his finger on it.

"K.C...." Katy began hesitantly as he took a sip from his glass. "I'm leaving." K.C. stopped in mid swallow and stared blankly into his glass. "I'm leaving Chicago for good," Katy continued, " ...and I want you to come with me."

K.C. wasn't totally surprised. He knew that the day would come that Katy would realize that she didn't belong there.

"I've got to get out of this place K.C.... I've got to go! You're like a brother to me I wouldn't feel right leaving you."

K.C. stood up from the table and walked silently into the adjoining living room. "I can't go with you Kat.... I love you... but I can't go with you."

"Why not?" she asked as she followed him into the living room. "We could go somewhere else! We could start new lives!"

K.C. turned to Katy with tears in his eyes. There was no new life for him he thought as he took her into his arms. "You do what you have to do," he whispered. "I just want you to be happy. I want you to be safe." He let Katy go and left the apartment.

Katy stood quietly in the window watching as K.C. disappeared up the street. She finally turned and went into her bedroom leaving the breakfast she'd prepared untouched on the dining room table. After a while she re-emerged from her room, cleared the table and washed the dishes. She went about the apartment cleaning and making busy work impatiently waiting for K.C. to come back. Two hours passed and still no sign of him. Finally Katy decided that she couldn't wait any longer. She got up from her bed and began to pack. She left the things that belonged to 'Kat' hanging in her closet. She wanted nothing else to do with 'Kat'. She wanted to be free of her and all the turmoil *she* had brought into her life.

In the bottom of her dresser drawer she found the red ribbon that her brother Kyle had given her. It was faded and dirty now just like she was. She wasn't that same cantankerous nine-year-old anymore. She was an 18-year-old whore. Older, but not necessarily wiser. Katy put the ribbon on her pillow and continued packing. As she moved about her room she heard the harmonious sounds coming from the church on the corner through an open window. It was Sunday morning and even if she felt she was not welcomed to go in, she could enjoy it from afar.

After she finished packing Katy sat down with a pad of paper and penned a note to K.C.:

To my dear friend,

By the time you read this letter I will be gone. It seems that I have known you all my life. You are the dearest man and the dearest friend that I could have ever hoped for. In the short time that I've known you, you have seen me through some really bad times and I am grateful to you for being there. Although I don't exactly know where I will go from here I wish that I could have convinced you to go with me. This is not goodbye. I will see you again soon and hopefully by then I would have been able to pull my life together, at least whatever life I can squeeze out of what's left of me. I will send you some money as soon as I get settled and find a job. The rent has been paid through the end of next month. I hate to leave you like this but if I don't get out of Chicago and away from Sugar Man I'm going to die. Please, please take care of yourself. I would hate myself if anything ever happened you. Stay strong.

I love you,

Kat

Katy wiped the tears from her eyes with the back of her hand, folded the note and sealed it in an envelope. She then took the faded ribbon from her pillow and tied it around the envelope. Katy grabbed her jacket, suitcase, and purse and went into the living room. She propped the envelope up against a lamp on the table facing the door and looked solemnly around the room. "Take care of yourself," she whispered. Making sure she had everything Katy opened her purse and counted the money she had left. There was $350, $50 of which she took from her purse and laid next to the letter. "I'll miss you K.C.," she said as she reached for the door. "But I won't miss this place."

When Katy opened the door she gasped in terror as she came face to face with Sugar Man.

"Where do you think you're goin'?" he leered as he laid against the door.

"W…When? H…How?" Katy stammered.

"You miss me baby?" Sugar Man oozed.

"How did you…" Katy continued.

"…Your old friend Earl," he injected cutting her off. "He's my lawyer. He got me off on account…"

"Account?" Katy inquired.

"On account of the fact that the judge likes doin' nasty things to little boys and takin' nasty pictures. Who would have guessed that the judge was such a freak!" he asked rhetorically. "What's the suitcase for?"

"I'm leaving!" Katy said indignantly.

"Leaving," he mocked. "Oh really?"

"I'm through with the street and I'm through with you!"

"Oh you think it's that easy huh? You just gonna walk out on me just like that?"

Sugar Man's even temperament troubled Katy but she would not relent.

"Yeah! Just like that!" she pressed.

Sugar Man adjusted his stance in the doorway and stretched his arms out across its frame.

"Oh I see how it is…Are you *saved* now? Is that it?" He laughed a low guttural laugh as he began to ridicule her. "You think cause that old man's been whisperin' in your ear about GOD that you can just pack up and leave… me." Katy shifted uneasily at the escalating anger in his voice. "You didn't think I knew about that did you? People talk Kat. I may have been locked up but I still kept my eye on you. If you leave me where you gonna go? What you gonna do? The only livin' you know how to make is on your back!" Sugar Man softened his tone and lowered his hands to caress Katy but she pulled away. "I made you little girl... The clothes on your back... The food you eat... I even gave you your name... The only reason you exist is because Sugar said so... Besides, you know Sugar Man is the only somebody that is gonna take care of you...and you know that there ain't no place you can go that I won't find you."

"Oh yeah," Katy said daringly. "JUST WATCH ME!!!"

Katy pulled the door to the apartment closed, pushed past Sugar Man on the staircase and bolted out of the building, undaunted he ran after her. As she reached the sidewalk Sugar Man caught up to her, threw his arms around her to try and prevent her from moving as she struggled to pull free.

"GET OFF ME!!!" Katy yelled.

"You owe me!" Sugar Man sniped. "You owe me big time!"

"I don't owe you nothin'!" Katy retorted as she bucked like a wild cat in an attempt to loosen his grip on her.

Realizing that her resistance was too much for him to control, Sugar Man let her go and grabbed her purse. She grabbed at him trying to get it back but he held her at bay. He pushed her hard enough for her to loose her balance, and stumble over her suitcase, then fall to the ground. Sugar Man opened her purse and dumped its contents on the sidewalk. He picked up the $300 that she had left and put it into his pocket as she jumped up from the ground and attacked him again. Katy slapped him hard across the face and he sent her flying into the side of the brick building.

"Now let's see you try to get out of town without money!" he snapped as he straightened his clothes. "You think about what you're doin' girl do you hear? Life would be a whole lot better with me than with some GOD that you can't even see!"

As Katy lay on the sidewalk whimpering Sugar Man opened her suitcase and dumped it's contents on the ground next to her.

"When you come to your senses you know where to find me!"

He shook the empty suitcase as if he expected more to fall out then tossed it aside as he sauntered to his car and raced off. The tenants in the building who witnessed Sugar Man's brutality made no attempt to get involved. They simply moved away from their windows and went about their business. As Katy pulled herself together the church bells rang out signifying the end of service. She rose up off the ground, and put her things in order as Speed rounded the corner at the end of the block. The sound of the church bells was deafening but could not mask the unmistakable blast of gunfire. Speed was hit square in the back and again in the head. As Katy tried to duck for cover she too was hit. The first bullet hit her in the leg and a second bullet hit her in the chest. This new commotion brought one of the neighbors screaming back to her window. Pandemonium erupted, as other bystanders ran screaming for protection.

K.C., who was a half a block away on his way back to the apartment, heard the shots but didn't think anything of it until he rounded the corner of the street where his building was.

"Kat!" K.C. screamed as he pushed through the crowd that gathered. "NO!!!" he screamed as he got closer. It was as if he were caught in a nightmare. He knelt beside Katy's lifeless body and tenderly picked up her head. Tears stung his skin as they streamed down his face and he cried, "HELP ME! PLEASE SOMEBODY HELP ME!"

The crowd made no move to assist him. They all just watched as he cradled her head and rocked back and forth on his knees. Suddenly one of the women from the church broke through the throng of people and ran towards K.C. "Call an ambulance!" she shrieked. It was one of the women who had walked up that street a hundred times before. One of the same women that snubbed her nose at K.C. and Katy when she'd seen them on the street. One of the same women who looked at them in disdain as she hurried to pass and to get to her church to serve her God. The older of the two, was directly on her heels trying to stop her but she was unable to hold her.

"Lord Jesus look like the whole world done gone crazy!" she shouted as she threw up her hands in defeat.

The woman who had pushed forward first attended to Speed, as K.C. was reluctant to let her get near Katy. The woman took Speed's small inanimate hand in hers and checked for signs of life. She held back the urge to cry out as she saw that a bullet had pierced his skull and his eyes were still open. Despite herself tears began to run down her face. His blood-covered face was so innocent, she thought, he was so young. The woman passed her hand over his eyes and closed them as she got up from her kneeling position to attend to Katy.

"Don't touch her!" K.C. screamed as he pushed the woman violently away.

"Go make sure that ambulance finds us!" she shouted back at K.C.

"What are you doing?... Leave her alone!" he screamed in a panic.

"I'm a nurse!" she responded. "I'm going to try to help her!"

"Leave her alone! Go see about him!" K.C. said pointing to Speed's body.

The woman closed her eyes as if praying and quietly said, "He's dead. Now go make sure that ambulance finds us before we lose her too...GO!" she shouted.

K.C. sprang to his feet wiping his blood covered hands on his clothes and ran toward the sound of the sirens blaring in the distance. The crowd was ominously silent as they watched the nurse put her mouth to Katy's mouth in an attempt to breathe life back into her. She had broken through the walls and abandoned the invisible barriers that had separated the prosperous from the poor, the streets from the church, the saints from the sinners. The woman had given little regard to the new dress she had purchased for that particular Sunday meeting. Oddly it wasn't the fact that she was a nurse that had led the woman to such a heroic feat, it was GOD Himself who compelled her.

24

The rain was coming down in torrents, which left the streets of Chicago virtually empty with the exception of the few brave souls that dared to venture out. The sound of the rain pounding the pavement was like a battalion of foot soldiers charging into battle, but Tee and her male companion were oblivious to it all. They sat in an alley wedged in the doorway of an abandoned building for shelter against the elements. They were getting high and laughing as if they didn't have a care in the world. Tee was due to deliver any day and should have been making preparations for the birth but there were none. She acted as if there were no baby at all, as if there were no pregnancy. Her lover kept her mind sedate and occupied so much so that she barely knew where she was half the time. That thin cylinder of glass with the balled tip that she clung to for life was the only thing she was conscious of. Her next high was the only thing that mattered and she would do anything to get it.

"One for me," Tee said laughing as she inhaled deeply. "And one for the bastard... I mean baby," as she inhaled again. She laughed callously as if she intentionally meant to do herself harm and her companion laughed too. He didn't care enough about himself to be concerned about Tee or her condition.

Tee awkwardly pulled herself up from her sitting position and lackadaisically danced her way out into the storm. "Hush little baby don't say a word," she began in a singsong manner. "Mama's gonna buy you a mockingbird—and if that mockingbird don't sing, mama's gonna buy you a...mama's gonna buy you a..." Tee started to strain and contract as a spasm of pain ripped through her body. She doubled over and fell to her knees as she let go of an ear-piercing scream. The man that was with her snapped to attention watching her body writhing in the alley as the rain continued to fall. "Help me!" she screamed reaching out for her companion. The man only stumbled to his feet and ran away from her. Tee was left in the alley, in the dark, alone.

The excruciating pain sharpened Tee's senses as she struggled to pull herself back into the doorway. Tee was soaked through to her skin and even in her anesthetized state she knew what was happening to her. She had been down this road twice before, she knew that the baby was coming and there was nothing she could do to stop it. She bit her bottom lip and panted as one contraction gave way to another. Her screams of pain rang out into the darkness and dissipated into the thunderous rain. Tee could feel her entire body convulsing as the being inside of her thrust forward. She released another vacuous howl as she realized that she would have to deliver the baby on her own. Tee wriggled free of her pants and pulled off her wet jacket. She placed her jacket in a box for padding as she straddled atop the makeshift nest. Once in position Tee squeezed her eyes shut and braced herself in the doorframe. Everything she learned up until now had prepared her for that moment. The birth of Brandy and Byron, and the things that she learned in high school biology, and on all those endless medical programs she watched on television, she felt had more than prepared her for this. "I can do this," Tee hissed through her clenched teeth as she took one cleansing breath after the other. How bizarre she looked on her knees trembling and bracing as pain shot through her like fire. After several minutes of tortuous agony every fiber of her being tensed and Tee discharged one final shout as the head crowned and the baby shot forth from the birth canal. Tee was weak from her efforts and her breathing was labored but she felt an amazing sense of liberation. She collapsed on the ground beside the box where the baby lay still attached to the umbilical cord. When she regained her composure she gently put her hand into the box and wrapped her coat around the tiny little creature and picked it up. She could tell right away that she had given birth to a son. She could also see that the tiny bluish wrinkled mucous covered figure was not crying. As the storm slowly quieted to the west of her Tee brushed her hand across its tiny mouth but there was no breath. She then cautiously pressed her hand to his small chest but there was no heart beat. Tee's throat tightened as she closed her eyes and pulled her baby into her. She leaned her head back on the wall behind her and sat sullenly without words, without tears, without remorse.

When Tee opened her eyes she carefully placed the baby back in the box and scanned the area where she sat for something with which to cut the umbilical cord. She reached for a shard of glass a few feet away from her and methodically freed herself from the attachment of death. Blood was everywhere but Tee cleaned up her mess as best she could. She struggled back into her wet jeans and took the dead baby wrapped in her jacket and threw it into a nearby dumpster. On the other side of the alley she found a stack of newspapers which she used along with the standing rainwater to clean herself. With her strength waning Tee slumped against the dumpster for support and fell to her knees. She was just about to lose consciousness when she saw a rat scampering through the alley. She clumsily pulled herself up and staggered the opposite way up the alley pulling the sweatshirt she had on over her hands and entwining her arms around her chest willing herself not to fall.

It was three o'clock in the morning by the time Tee made her way back to the halfway house, but the doors were locked. She stood there barely enough strength to knock and collapsed.

* * * * * * * * *

Tee heard voices calling out to her from amidst the fog of her delirium. "Tee wake up!" "Tee do you know where you are? Can you hear me?" "Tee where is the baby?" "What did you do with the baby?" Tee heard all the voices but it was as if they were talking to somebody else. She felt suspended somewhere between life and death, between heaven and hell. She was there but she wasn't. Everything seemed so surreal, as if she were in a time warp. But it was one voice in particular that pierced through the blackness. "Thelma...Thelma it's your mother. Wake up! Wake up! Do you hear me!" In her mind, Tee was back in another time and she heard her mother's voice waking her up for school. Her eye's sprung open at the illusion of her mother's beckoning call. Her mouth opened and she formed the word "Mama," but there was no sound.

"Do you know where you are?"

Tee looked up into the face of Rachel Porter, the woman who ran the halfway house. "Tee can you understand me?"

Tee nodded her head but she still didn't speak.

"Tee you're in the hospital," Ms. Porter continued. "Do you want me to call your mother?"

Tee closed her eyes slightly and shook her head.

"Tee the police have been here. They want to know where the baby is."

Tee instinctively touched her abdomen and she opened her eyes and glared vacantly at the woman. "The baby is dead," she whispered.

The woman's cheeks flexed and she blew a quiet breath out before continuing. "Tee, did something happen that you want to tell me about? Did you do something to your baby?" Tee turned away from the woman and faced the wall. "The police are talking murder, or at the very least felony abandonment. You could be facing some very severe implications here." Becoming frustrated at Tee's lack of attention the woman grabbed Tee's face and turned it back to face her. "Tee, where is the baby? You were in bad shape when we found you. We know that you had to have just given birth. Please tell me where the baby is so I can help you."

Tee remained silent. The impatience of the woman was apparent. She let go of Tee's face grabbed her purse and quietly left the room.

Tee didn't much care about the legal ramifications of her actions. She didn't care what the police charged her with or what they did to her. She was tired of living the way she had been and any change, she felt, would have been for the better. After a few days in the hospital Tee slipped away from the watchful eye of Rachel Porter and curiously returned to the alley where she had dumped the body of her dead baby. She didn't expect to find it there after so long a time but what she did find waiting for her was just as startling as anything else.

It was late in the afternoon and as she approached the dumpster she saw Old Ben pushing his a rickety shopping cart up the alley in her direction. The closer he got to her she could hear that he was singing. *"...I once was lost but now I'm found...was blind...but now...I see."* He stopped when he reached her and stared knowingly into her eyes. "It's time Tee."

"Time for what?" Tee snapped.

"Time for you to stop running...Time for you stop hiding."

"I'll tell you what its time for old man...It's time for you to leave me alone! That's what its time for!"

"Don't let your baby's death eat away at you."

Tee, who had turned her back on Old Ben, turned sharply around to face him. Although verbally she admitted nothing, her body language confessed the truth. She was noticeably agitated and fidgety.

"I don't know what you're talkin' about!" Tee said angrily. "You're crazy!"

Without looking away from her Old Ben reached into his shopping cart and retrieved the blood stained jacket that Tee had disposed of along with her baby. Tee's countenance flushed and her eyes widened.

"This does belong to you doesn't it?" Old Ben asked as though he already knew the answer to the question.

"Where did you get that?" Tee questioned nervously as she pulled at her hair.

"You were in a lot a pain," Old Ben continued. "You still are. You feel like you've been abandoned and you're alone but you're not. What you did was very serious. There will be repercussions..."

"...So what else is new!" Tee interrupted.

"Birthing something into the world does not come without pain...Just ask GOD," Old Ben continued holding up the coat to her. "This blood is the evidence of life, just as Jesus' shed blood is the evidence of eternal life," Old Ben said as he buried the coat deep into the cart. "This blood was shed for a reason..." As he continued to speak he pulled the bible out of the cart that he had once given to Katy and presented it to Tee. "...So was His."

If he had her coat, he must know something about the baby, Tee thought but was afraid to ask.

"Everything you've been through," Old Ben pressed. "Everything that happened was ordained by GOD. He wants to work something in you that will be a magnet for others just like you. GOD put you to the test to give you a *testimony*. Everything you went through and will yet go through would have driven somebody else crazy but you are stronger than you think you are. Giving birth to that baby by yourself proved that. GOD has His hand on you Tee you know what that feels like and its scares you. *Before I formed you in the womb I knew you. Before you were born I set you apart.* GOD is for you Tee and if He's for you this thing *cannot* destroy you. Trust GOD to make a way."

It seemed that they stood and talked in the alley for hours. One of the things he said prompted Tee to go back and try again with her mother. As she walked up the block to the building that her mother lived in Tee could see a group of children playing on the sidewalk... Brandy was among them. Tee stopped, sat down on the stoop of a neighboring building, and watched them. Brandy was laughing and skipping rope and playing as if everything in her world was as it should be. Brandy seemed untouched by the absence of her mother Tee thought, but then again she had Rosetta to look after her. Eventually Tee mustered the courage to get up from the stoop and crossed the street. As she approached the building Brandy saw her and ran in to get Rosetta. The other children stopped playing long enough to look at Tee as she ascended the stairs into the building. How strange she must have looked to them. Her hair was unkempt, she had no makeup on, and her clothing was anything the shelter had provided courtesy of the Salvation Army. Even as poor as she felt she had been all her life, she had never looked or felt so low.

It was Sunday; Tee could smell the makings of one of Rosetta's delicious dinners as she continued up the stairs. "Maybe mama will let me come home," Tee thought. "Maybe she will let me stay for dinner." When she reached the landing her heart was aflutter, as she could not imagine how she would be received. Tee straightened her clothes and ran her hands through her tangled hair to make herself more presentable. Tee raised her hand to knock on the door and found it ajar. She stepped inside to find Rosetta standing there with Brandy hiding behind her as if she needed protection.

"Brandy go next door to see if Miss Lucinda got some flour I can borrow," Rosetta said as she coaxed Brandy to the door.

When Brandy started for the door Tee stooped down to stop her so that she could get a better look at her. Brandy shrank in fear and backed away. Realizing that her daughter was afraid of her Tee backed away.

"Go on next door Brandy and do what I told you," Rosetta repeated. Brandy quickly left and closed the door behind her. Rosetta, still dressed in her church clothes, wiped her hands on her apron and moved to the sofa, anxiously fussing with the cushions. "What are you doing here Tee," she asked sternly.

Tee stood before her as if she was no older than Brandy resisting the urge to fall down on her face and beg her mother to forgive her and let her come back home. She had not been high since the night she gave birth and the withdrawal put her on the edge. Tee inhaled deeply and quietly said, "I wanna come home."

"This ain't your home no more," Rosetta said as she stopped fussing with the sofa cushions and stood up. "You made your bed, now you go lie in it...You and whatever trifling and sorry two-legged mongrel you happen to be with these days. You've lied to me before. Why should I believe you now? Why should this time be any different?"

"I'm not lying now," Tee cried as tears began to fall in spite of her resolve. "I just wanna come home! I'm tired...I just wanna come home and start over."

"Yeah well I'm tired too Tee," Rosetta retorted angrily. "I'm tired of you comin' in here with the same old mess just long enough to steal enough money so you can go right back out in the street and do the same stuff over again! I can't take it no more Tee...No more do you hear me!"

"It's different this time mama I swear," Tee anguished as she stood trembling in the wake of her mother's rebuke.

"It's always different Tee," Rosetta exclaimed throwing her hands up and moving into the kitchen to check on dinner. A few minutes later Rosetta re-emerged with the question that Tee had waited for her to ask. "Where's the baby," she said pointing to her stomach.

"Dead," Tee responded flatly.

Rosetta gasped and put her hand to her mouth, she had not been prepared for Tee's honesty. Her insides were a tumult but she didn't want Tee to see her break.

"The baby is dead!" Tee repeated more vehemently. "Are you happy now mama?"

Rosetta stilled herself as she began to pace the floor. "Well no better for you," she shouted. "You got two now that you can't take care of...Like pastor always says...YOU ARE CURSED WITH A CURSE!" Rosetta stopped momentarily frustrated that she had taken a scripture about tithing and so foolishly used it out of context. "He judged you that's why you're in this mess...Now you wanna come home...and do what? Mess up these other children's lives? Well I ain't havin' it! You hear me! You ain't bringin' that mess in my house! GOD help me if Brandy grows up to be anything like you turned out to be!"

Brandy slipped back in the door unnoticed and heard the last of Rosetta's outburst against her mother. The two women just stood there inches from each other as if one was waiting for the other to speak. Tee slowly moved toward Rosetta and Rosetta drew back as if preparing for a fight, but Tee had no fight left.

Instead she reached for her mother and embraced her tightly. Tee held onto Rosetta as if hoping to pull down the wall between them, but she finally gave up and started for the door. Tee looked and saw Brandy, and Brandy looked at her with her big doe eyes and watched her mother leave the house without so much as another word. After Tee left Rosetta slowly sat down on the sofa, buried her face in her hands, and cried. Brandy's heart was pricked and she moved to her grandmother and put her arm around her shoulder. "It's all right Gran," she said quietly. "Don't cry...It's all right."

* * * * * * * * *

Ms. Porter and Tee's court appointed attorney accompanied her to court for judgement day. Tee actually seemed like her old self as she sat nervously in the courtroom waiting for her case to be called. The fact that she had been in trouble with the law before was going to weigh heavily on the judge's decision as well as the fact that she had been in and out of the halfway house and hadn't maintained her drug treatment program. The disappearance of the baby was going to be a factor as well. Although the body was eventually discovered and an autopsy determined that the baby was stillborn, with no evidence of foul play, Tee was liable for the child and her blatant disregard for its safety.

"Case number 165798 the state of Illinois versus Thelma Renee Dennis," echoed the booming voice of the bailiff as he called the court to order.

The state presented its case and the defense gave its stirring rebuttal as Tee sat solemn and stone-faced through it all. It wasn't until an unexpected witness for the defense stepped into the courtroom that Tee's demeanor changed. The state was of course resistant but the judge overruled any objections and asked Rosetta for her testimony. Rosetta stepped forward with all the dignity and grace that she could muster and sat before the courtroom as the room fell silent. Rachel Porter had called Rosetta several days before and made an impassioned plea for her to help save her daughter's life before she got lost in an uncaring system and all hope for recovery would be gone forever.

"Your honor," Rosetta began as she cleared her throat. "My daughter Thelma is admittedly a drug user, but it was the generations of sin in my family that drove her to it. If I could take back any day in my life it would be the day that I turned my back on Tee after I found out that she was raped... by my son."

Humiliation and disgrace filled Rosetta as tears flowed down her cheeks like a waterfall. As she continued unfolding the sordid history of her family the heart of the entire courtroom gave ear to her anguish. Tee was crying, Ms. Porter was crying, and despite herself the judge was crying. It was the first time in her life that Rosetta had given voice to the curse that she had unleashed upon her family. It was the first time she was willing to admit that there was such a thing.

"I know that you have to do what you have to do," Rosetta concluded. "But just know that no matter what Tee has done I love her. She's my daughter. I love her. I will do what ever I have to do to help her pull her life back together. Please your honor I beg you not to lock her up, give her a chance to break free of the hell that I helped to put her in. She needs GOD, she doesn't need a jail cell. GOD is the only one that can make my daughter whole."

Rosetta's words were eloquent and full of conviction and the judge was so moved that she could not continue. She called for a brief recess in order to pull herself together and the courtroom was adjourned. Tee sat unable to move for the longest time. She never knew some of the things her mother had revealed about her family in such a public forum. She never knew the shame and degradation that Rosetta had to live with all her life. She never knew that she was really loved. Tee got up from the table where she sat and moved swiftly to her mother and threw her arms around her. Rosetta returned Tee's embrace and the two held on to each other as if there were no one else in the world.

Tee was charged with abandonment and given a three year suspended sentence under the stipulation that she would undergo a comprehensive psychiatric evaluation and mandatory drug treatment program. Tee was ordered to live in the rehab center for a period of one year with periodic checkups by a court appointed physician. She would be given a strict curfew and if not adhered to for any reason she would be remanded to the custody of the Cook County Correctional facility in Cook County, Illinois.

* * * * * * * * *

As Tee prepared to spend the first night in her room at the rehab center she remembered the profound words of the tattered old man in the alley. "GOD is for you Tee and if He's for you this thing *cannot* destroy you. Trust GOD to make a way." It was the first peaceful night of sleep that she'd had in a very long time.

25

After almost two weeks of death like sleep Katy finally opened her eyes and looked around the room to find K.C.'s elongated body uncomfortably stretched across a chair. Her body remained immobile as her eyes frantically scanned her surroundings. She was disoriented and confused as she tried to recall what had happened. "Hospital," she thought unable to speak because of the tubing attached to her mouth helping her breathe. "I'm not dead," she thought again as a single tear flowed down her face from the corner of her eye. One of the bullets that hit Katy pierced her left lung coming dangerously close to her heart but after several hours of surgery the doctors were able to repair the extensive damage that had been caused. It wasn't enough that she was already slightly anemic but during the surgery Katy's blood pressure shot up so high she suffered a mild stroke. It had been touch and go for a while but the doctors gave her a fighting chance. Katy could swear that just as she stepped into the unknown she could hear her brother Kyle saying, "Go back! Go back! It's not time yet."

The door opened and light flooded into the room. "Well look who's finally awake," the night nurse whispered as she crept into the room. She quietly checked all the machines and the monitors as well as the intravenous bags that kept a constant supply of medicine and nutrients flowing into Katy's comatosed body. "That young man over there is going to be real happy to see you," she beamed. "He's barely left this place since you got here you know." The nurse made several notations on the chart at the foot of Katy's bed and after she was certain that Katy could breathe on her own she removed the tube from her mouth.

"Would you like a little water sweetheart?" she said in a comforting tone. Katy nodded and the nurse poured a small amount into a cup. "Not too fast now," chided the nurse as she assisted Katy. "Is that better?" Katy nodded again. "Should I wake up your young friend?" Katy opened her mouth to speak and the word "yes" squeaked out.

K.C. stirred in the chair as the nurse shook him awake. He stretched his long legs in one direction and his arms in another and made a deep yawning noise. The nurse tilted her head in Katy's direction and K.C.'s face lit up as he saw that she was finally awake.

"Don't keep her too long baby," said the nurse as she walked towards the door. "And you," she directed to Katy. "No talkin' you hear."

K.C. moved to the edge of Katy's bed and gently took her hand. Katy squeezed his hand for reassurance and despite himself K.C. teared up.

Katy painfully cleared her throat. She couldn't help it she had to say something. "So much for me getting out of Chicago," she said in a low raspy whisper. "Are you all right?"

"I've got something to tell you," K.C. began. "...and I don't want you to be upset."

Katy's eyebrows furrowed with concern as K.C. pressed on.

"Do you remember what happened to you?" Katy nodded but her eyes registered confusion. "You were shot," K.C. continued. "Do you remember that?" Katy nodded again. "Speed got shot too...he didn't make it though... I thought you were gonna to die too...so... I called your father."

Katy opened her mouth to speak and shook her head. She didn't want her father to come, not now. She was so ashamed of what she had become she didn't know if she would be able to look at him. "No K.C.," she whispered. "No."

"Don't worry," K.C. injected trying to calm her down. "I didn't tell him anything except that you got shot. Kat, I..." Just as K.C. was about to go on the door opened again. Katy's eyes widened with amazement as she made eye contact with her father.

K.C. got up from the bed and moved to the window as Kyle came into the room. It was obvious that he too had been there for a long time—waiting. His clothes were wrinkled, his hair was disheveled and his eyes were red and bloodshot. He apprehensively walked to Katy's bedside and picked her up in his arms like he did when she was a very little girl. Katy was at first resistant thinking that he would see right through her, thinking that he would somehow be able to tell. But in the comfort of her father's arms once more none of that seemed to matter.

"I thought I had lost you too," he cried. "Thank GOD you're all right."

GOD, Katy mused. In her whole life she never heard her father call the name of GOD unless it was followed by an inflammatory remark. She was so dumbfounded by his appearance that she scarcely knew what to say or how to react.

"This young man called me and told me that you had been shot…How in the…No…It's not important…The important thing is that you're all right… I have been out of my mind with worry." Kyle said letting Katy go. "I don't know how you ever got to this horrible place but I swear to you that I will not let you stay here. As soon as you're able to travel I'm going to fly you back to Youngstown and get you the best medical attention that money can buy. No daughter of mine is going to be subjected to such squalid conditions. Tomorrow morning I'm going to…"

"STOP!" Katy gasped as she squeezed her eyes shut and tried to find the strength to talk. "I'm not going anywhere with you." Each word was harder and harder for her to choke out but there were things that had to be said. She had to press through the pain. "You have no idea what has happened to me over this past year. I am not the same naïve little simpleton that I used to be. I've grown up dad and I did it without the comfort of your wallet. You weren't there to make it all better. In fact every time I tried to call you, you refused to talk to me. And now you want to come in here and put on this…this act! You have a lot of nerve!" Katy fell back into the pillow swallowed painfully and took a deep breath.

"Let's not talk about this now…You need your strength. We can talk more when you feel better," Kyle said quietly.

"I want to talk about this now," Katy winced. "You went off and married that witch, cut me off financially, and turned your back on me to pay me back…Why did you come here dad? So you can soothe your guilty conscience?" The inflection in Katy's voice rose and fell in squeaks and whispers as anger rekindled inside her.

Kyle flushed with embarrassment as he steadied himself to be castigated by his daughter. He turned to K.C. and asked if he would leave them alone to talk but Katy would have none of it.

"K.C. is my friend!" she protested. "He has been more like family to me than you have!"

"I don't want to fight Katy. I was wrong, terribly, terribly wrong for what I did to you. I never meant for things to get so out of control between us. I had hoped that you would have come to your senses about this character that you had attached yourself to and come home. I know that I was wrong about not telling you about my marriage to Helen, that was a mistake, and as it turns out, so was my marriage to Helen. But that doesn't excuse the way I handled this situation. My behavior has been appalling but I can't correct the past. I can only hope to make it all up to you now. I can only imagine the horrors that you have had to endure all these months and I will go to my grave asking for your forgiveness. Come home Katy…Please."

Kyle was more honest with Katy in that moment than he had ever been. And Katy could see it in his eyes. Katy reached out to her father and he swept her up in his arms and sobbed. In the midst of their tender moment K.C. slipped out the door unnoticed and rang the elevator. "I look like crap," he said as he stepped inside the elevator and saw his reflection on the closing doors. As the elevator descended from floor to floor K.C. saw something else that disturbed him. Through the open buttons of his shirt he noticed that a lesion had formed at the nape of his neck. He opened his shirt up exposing more of his chest and discovered that there were more of them that had formed. "No

GOD... No!" he cried as he fell back against the wall of the elevator. He wanted to get drunk. He wanted to get high. He just wanted to escape but he didn't have any money. Demoralized, K.C. found himself standing on the bus stop right outside the hospital asking for spare change from anyone who happened by. It was 10:30 at night, by midnight K.C. had collected almost thirty dollars. He hopped a bus and headed for home. He got off the bus and stood in contemplation for a minute before he crossed the street and went into the liquor store.

"Hey K.C., how's it goin'? Sorry about that girlfriend of yours that got herself shot!" yelled Popps the storeowner as K.C. walked in. K.C. waved an acknowledgement to the man behind the counter and then proceeded down the aisle where the vodka was kept. On his better days K.C. would sometimes hang out at the liquor store and play chess with Popps but he wasn't in a chess-playing mood this night.

"That was the boy that was livin' with that white girl down the street ain't it?" asked another patron standing at the counter conversing with Popps. He appeared to be trying to whisper but his efforts were ineffective. "My ol' lady that lives in that buildin' says she saw who did it you know?" When the man said that K.C.'s ears were pricked and he became more attentive all the while pretending to peruse the aisles as he went along.

"Why didn't yo' ol' lady say somethin' to the police?" whispered Popps.

"Are you kiddin' me, then she'd be takin' a dirt nap just like that kid...Sally may be crazy but she ain't stupid."

"So who'd she say she saw?" Popps inquired.

"She said that the white girl was fightin' with Sugar Man and the next thing you know he speeds off in that little red Mercedes of his. A few minutes later she looks up the alley and who does she see racin' through with his gun aimed at that kid."

"Naw," Popps replied in disbelief.

"If I'm lyin' may GOD strike me dead right here!" Popps took a step back expecting lightening to strike the man unfolding his tale and then he curiously leaned back in to hear its conclusion.

"He shot that boy right through the head," the man continued. "Then he shot that white girl...Everybody made it sound like it was one of them gangs doin' a *drive by* or somethin'. It was a *drive by* all right, and Sugar Man was doin' the drivin'."

K.C. saw red as he grabbed the least expensive fifth of vodka on the shelf and headed for the counter.

"You all right son?" Popps inquired. "You look a little green around the gills."

"Yeah I'm fine Popps, just fine!" K.C. seethed as he retrieved his change and headed out the door.

"You don't think he heard me do you Popps?" asked the man at the counter looking nervously through the window at K.C. running across the street.

"What do you think Fred," Popps sneered. "You don't exactly know how to whisper."

"Well what do you think he's gonna do?"

"Your guess is as good as mine."

* * * * * * * * *

Old Ben was standing on the street corner preaching and spouting scriptures to passersby when Cookie came out of her apartment building. She had come out to wait for Sugar Man and she was all done up in one of her most provocative outfits. When she spotted Old Ben on the corner she decided to provoke him while she waited.

"I am the way...The truth...and the life," Old Ben spouted. "No man comes to the Father but by me...Behold I set before you this day good and evil...Life and death...Choose Life!"

"What are you over here mumblin' about old man?" Cookie teased as she pulled a wad of cash from her bra and fanned it in front of Old Ben's weathered face. "*This* is life! With this I can buy me a better life! Sugar is gonna take good care of me!"

Undaunted Old Ben pushed Cookie's hand from in front of his face. "When the wicked man dies, his expectation will perish, and the hope of the unjust perishes."

"Save it!" Cookie jeered. "All that bible thumpin' don't work on me like it did on Kat. Why don't you go find somebody else to save!"

"Justin," Old Ben said as his eyes narrowed and he looked directly into Cookie's eyes.

"What did you say?" Cookie asked warily.

"Is Justin worth savin'?" he pressed. "That's the name that you have tattooed on your left arm... It's sad ain't it?... Every son should know his mother."

Cookie backed away from him as the wheels of Sugar Man's car screeched up the street. He parked the car and jumped out grabbing Cookie and kissing her passionately in front of Old Ben. "You got my money baby," he cooed as he slapped her on her rear. Cookie took the wad of bills and handed them to Sugar Man and he put them in his money clip and back in his pocket. He then turned to open the passenger side door for Cookie and she hesitantly got in. When he closed the door Cookie looked back at Old Ben who had not taken his eyes off of her.

"You stay away from Cookie you hear me old man!" Sugar Man said demandingly. "I don't want you fillin' her head with all that crap about love and forgiveness, and life! You already cost me Kat!" He reached into the car and kissed Cookie seductively on the neck. "This one's all mine!"

Suddenly from behind him K.C. pulled his arm, swung him around, and punched him in the mouth with every ounce of strength he could muster. The force of K.C's punch caused Sugar Man to slide across the freshly waxed hood of his car and fall to the ground. Cookie jumped out of the car and ran to help him up.

"GET UP!...GET UP!" K.C. stammered.

"You drunk son of a..." Sugar Man hissed. "Have you lost your mind?"

"It was you!" K.C. yelled. "It was you that killed Speed! It was you that shot Kat! It was you!"

Cookie was horrified and pulled away from Sugar Man as he leaned on her while pulling himself off the ground.

"So what if it was you little punk," Sugar Man said as he removed a handkerchief from the pocket of his jacket and wiped the blood from his mouth. What are you gonna do about it! I don't care what you heard, you can't prove nothin!"

K.C. was wildly agitated as he pulled a gun from the small of his back and pointed it at Sugar Man.

"K.C. don't!" Old Ben yelled as he lunged toward K.C.

"You better listen to the old man!" Sugar Man chided.

"Give me the gun K.C." Old Ben pleaded.

There was a long silence as K.C. swayed back and forth with the gun still trained on Sugar Man's head. Sweat formed on K.C.'s brow and ran down his face, stinging his eyes, causing him to wince. Sugar Man seized the opportunity to sucker punch K.C. He flew one way and the gun flew another. Old Ben and Sugar Man lunged for the gun at the same time but Sugar Man was too quick for him. Sugar Man grabbed the gun and put it to K.C.'s temple.

"Back off old man!" he shouted. "I will kill him...make no mistake about that!"

"Go ahead!" K.C. insisted. "Do it! Pull the trigger!" K.C. started laughing and coughing simultaneously. Cookie didn't know what to make of it. "Go on kill me just like you did Speed! Put a bullet right through my head!" K.C.'s laughter became more hysterical. "But here's a little somethin' you might find funny though...I'm already dyin'! Ain't that a trip...I got AIDS!"

"You got AIDS!" Sugar Man repeated in disbelief. "You got AIDS and you hit me in my mouth!"

"Yeah," K.C. retorted. "I guess I'll see you in hell!"

Realizing that he had K.C.'s blood all over his hands and that it had been mixed with the blood on his mouth, Sugar Man lost it. He smacked K.C. in the head with the butt of the gun and knocked him out. "Have you lost your mind!" Cookie screamed as she violently pushed Sugar Man aside and rushed to aid her friend. Cookie showed no apprehension as she checked K.C.'s pulse and made sure that he was breathing despite his startling revelation.

"Cookie do you see what kind of man he is?" Old Ben injected. "He shot a little boy in the back! He put Kat in a coma...Is that how you want to end up? Kat thought this sorry excuse for a man was gonna take care of her too...She was wrong...Dead wrong!"

"Don't listen to him!" Sugar Man demanded. "He's just trying to mess with your head! He just wants you to turn into one of those church people! The same people," he continued directing his anger towards Old Ben, "that hung their so called *messiah* on the cross in the first place! RELIGIOUS BUZZARDS! They were looking for something that was right under their noses the whole time! Why would you want to be a part of that?"

Cookie didn't know what to make of Sugar Man's fanatical tirade. She looked at him as if she didn't know him.

"Religion never saved anybody!" Old Ben pressed. "Neither did being a part of a building and having your name on somebody's membership role ...The church is *me*...The church is *you*...Jesus knew HE was going to have to die when HE came here...that's why HE came...That's why HE died. The betrayal of the "religious buzzards" was all a part of His plan of salvation. It wasn't a mistake!" Old Ben looked tenderly at Cookie and continued, "You're not a mistake." He then looked angrily back at Sugar Man and proclaimed, "Neither are you!"

K.C. began to come around and Cookie helped him to his feet. He shook his head and staggered as he attempted to focus. Sugar Man reached out for Cookie and she pulled away from him. After she was sure that K.C. could stand on his own she let him go and approached Old Ben. "Who are you?" she inquired.

Old Ben looked lovingly into her eyes as he took her by the hand and continued. "All GOD wants from you Deborah is to be the best Deborah you can be...and you can only do that through Him...You don't need a pimp!...You need a savior!"

Cookie was stunned that he had called her by her given name. Tears inexplicably fell from her eyes as he spoke. "Who are you?" she inquired again.

"Who do you need me to be?" Old Ben responded.

Unable to listen to anymore Sugar Man pulled the two apart. "He's a nobody!" he shouted. "He's just a homeless bum! Don't listen to him!"

Anger raged inside Sugar Man as he unloaded the clip in the gun and violently threw it into the gutter. "You little fag! I should kill you anyway!" he directed at K.C. He then jumped into his car and revved the engine. "Get in the car!" he yelled at Cookie but she didn't move. "Did you hear me! I said get in the car!" Cookie shot Sugar Man an icy stare and turned and ran back into her building. Sugar Man cursed, slammed his fists into the dashboard of his car and tore up the street almost hitting a pedestrian.

After he was out of sight, K.C. sat down on the curb and wiped the blood from his mouth with the back of his hand. Old Ben who had been watching quietly sat down beside him.

"What are you going to do now?" Old Ben inquired staring off in the distance.

"I don't know old man," K.C. sneered. "Maybe I'll just go somewhere and die, would that satisfy you?"

Old Ben turned and looked at K.C. as empathy filled his heart and flooded into his eyes.

"What? No bible verses! No singin'! No preachin'! I know what you're thinkin', big deal right? I got what I deserved right? *GOD* is punishin' me for my sins. Maybe He is. Maybe I am gettin' what I deserve. Killin' my step father all those years ago is finally catchin' up to me. I have been tried and judged and the *"gay plague"* is my death sentence…Nobody can save me now."

"If you would stop beatin' yourself up long enough for GOD to work in you," Old Ben said quietly. "Maybe GOD can save you!"

"What's He gonna do!" K.C. sneered. "Make this all go away! Is He gonna *heal* me?"

"GOD can do anything He wants to do K.C.… GOD is sovereign."

K.C. looked at Old Ben as if he had heard the voice of Elizabeth Goldberg. Suddenly he was 13 again and he was sitting on that Greyhound bus headed for an uncertain future.

"GOD wants you to be free K.C.," Old Ben implored. "When this life is over, He wants to give you eternal life, no more suffering; no more beating; no more uncertainty. LIFE! Glorious LIFE! He wants to give you joy. GOD wants to give you peace. Do you know that in heaven there is no sickness? There is no death. There are no abusive men. There are no mother's that only care about you when they need you. There's only GOD and GOD is better than sex, or liquor, or any high. GOD *lasts forever!* Can you say that anything you've done up till now has lasted. You have sex...you're not satisfied. You drink...you end up feelin' sick or hung over...You get high and eventually you have to come down....You're empty K.C. GOD can fill that void for you if you let Him."

K.C. pulled a mangled cigarette from his pocket and broke off the bad piece and lit the stub. "I've got to get to the hospital," he said as he stood up. "Anything you want me to tell Kat?"

"Yes," Old Ben said softly. "Tell her, Jesus saves."

* * * * * * * * *

"Jesus saves," K.C. repeated as he slouched down on the seat in the back of the bus and laughed to himself. As the bus drove up the street he could see his reflection in the window caused by the glare of the afternoon sun. How haggard he looked, he thought to himself, how drawn, how pathetic. If it hadn't been for his eyes he would have scarcely recognized himself. He pulled his well-worn cap from the back pocket of his jeans and put it on. He squeezed his eyes shut and put his fingers to his throbbing temples. He then put on his sunglasses and buttoned his shirt all the way up. He scanned the faces of the hand full of passengers on the bus as one by one they continued to get on or off at their appointed stops. As they got closer to the hospital one passenger in particular boarded the bus that K.C. had not expected, his Aunt Gloria. Although she hadn't recognized him, K.C. knew who she was right away. The resemblance to his mother was unmistakable. Even though he had changed quite a bit since the last time they had seen each other he still felt uneasy as she made her way up the aisle to find a seat. A shiver ran down his spine and he wanted to go up to her and fall into her arms but fear kept him silent. It had been eight years, she probably believed that he murdered both his mother and his stepfather Warren, after all he did run. Maybe she even thought that he too was dead. Whatever he felt she thought, he would let her go on thinking it. He pulled the handle on the bus signifying that he wanted to get off and much to his surprise she was getting off too. He saw that she was dressed in a nurses uniform and panicked when he realized that she was working in the very hospital where Katy was. He'd been right up under her nose for days without knowing it. She stood at the front of the bus and he stood near the back. When she casually glanced around the bus before exiting he nervously bolted out of the rear. He ran towards the entrance to the hospital and disappeared through the revolving doors.

K.C. nervously watched over his shoulder as he waited impatiently for the elevator. Once the elevator doors opened he jumped in and frantically pressed the button as if to make the doors close faster. Just as the doors were about to close a hand reached in and caused the doors to spring open again. A knot formed in the pit of his stomach as he thought he was about to come face to face with his aunt.

"Whew! I thought I was going to miss it!" said the frenzied woman as she jumped into the elevator.

K.C. swallowed hard, closed his eyes, and fell back against the elevator wall when he realized that it was not his aunt. But he had seen her on the bus and he knew that she was somewhere in the hospital and he didn't want to take the chance of running into her.

****

When K.C. stepped off the elevator he ran into Kyle Sr. at the nurses station.

"Is Kat all right?" K.C. questioned.

"*Kat?*" Kyle repeated indignantly. "*Katy* is doing just fine. In fact she will be doing a whole lot better as soon as I get her out of this hospital and back to Youngstown."

Now that Katy was out of danger K.C. could see by looking at Kyle that everything that Katy told him about her father was true. He was an arrogant, self-righteous prig.

"I'm glad to see you young man," Kyle continued. "It will give us a chance to talk."

K.C. looked at Kyle and wondered what they could possibly have to talk about.

"Let's step over here shall we," Kyle said as he gestured towards the waiting area.

"I never got a chance to properly thank you for calling me and alerting me to my daughters situation, " he continued.

"You don't have to thank me," K.C. injected. "Kat means a lot to me. She's my family."

Kyle grimaced at K.C.'s comments and stared at him for several seconds before continuing. "Young man, I'm not going to mince words with you. I'm just going to lay it all out. My daughter has it in her head to get you to come back to Ohio with us and quite frankly I don't think that would be a good idea." Kyle put his hands in his pockets and began to pace as if he were presenting a case before a jury. "I can only imagine the kind of life and the kind of problems Katy has had living in this city but she needs to put it all behind her now, don't you agree?" Kyle looked sternly at K.C. who had leaned up against a windowsill and folded his arms. Kyle's demeanor did not intimidate K.C., he met Kyle's gaze eye to eye.

"Let me put your mind at ease Mr. Jennings," K.C. began. "First of all I don't think goin' back to Ohio with you is such a hot idea anyway for me or for *Katy*. But as far as she's concerned it's her decision to make. And its seems to me that she wouldn't have had *"this kind of life"* if you didn't turn your back on her when she needed you the most." K.C. unfolded his arms and started toward the exit. "Seems to me her problems started long before she got to Chicago." K.C. brushed passed Kyle and headed toward Katy's room.

K.C. tentatively opened the door to Katy's room and stuck his head inside.

"K.C." Katy said. "I'm not asleep. You can come in."

"How are you feelin'?" K.C. asked as he walked into the room.

Katy cleared her throat and answered that she felt better. K.C. sat gently on the side of her bed and they embraced.

"How are *you* feelin'?" Katy inquired.

"I feel great!" K.C. offered trying to sound up beat.

Katy lay back on her pillow and ran her hand over her friend's face. "What happened to your head?" she asked noticing the bruise inflicted by Sugar Man's gun.

"I fell down," K.C. responded. "Pretty clumsy, huh?"

She knew that something was wrong but she wanted him to tell her.

"I'm going back to Ohio when I get out of here," Katy said. "Will you consider coming with me?"

K.C. got up from the bed and walked over to the window. "Kat I told you before that I didn't want to go with you. I can't. Besides what would I do in a place like Youngstown, Ohio."

"You could live," Katy responded.

"It's not for me!"

"Why not?"

"Because... Because I have AIDS that's why not!"

The blood drained from Katy's face at the realization of what she suspected was true.

"I don't want to go to Ohio to die," K.C. said. "I can die just fine right here in Chicago."

K.C. started to cry but he kept his face toward the window to keep Katy from seeing. Katy too had started crying. Now that her suspicions were confirmed she had no idea what to say to K.C. or how to comfort him.

"Everything all right in here?" Kyle inquired as he walked into the room.

K.C. quickly wiped the tears from his eyes and cleared his throat. The room fell solemn. Kyle looked at K.C. who had not turned around and then he looked at the stricken look on his daughter's face.

"Katy are you all right?" he asked as he moved to her bedside.

"Daddy," Katy began as she rubbed her eyes. "How much cash do you have on you?"

Katy's question surprised Kyle and caused K.C. to turn and look at her.

"A couple of hundred dollars," Kyle stammered. "Why?"

"I want you to give it to K.C." she responded.

"No Kat!" K.C. objected as he moved to Katy's opposite side.

"Yes!" Katy demanded looking at her friend. "You're not working right now. You need to eat. You need to take care of yourself."

Kyle looked at K.C. as if he had put Katy up to asking for the money.

"K.C. didn't ask for any money daddy!" she injected interpreting his look. "We lived together. I'm not going to leave him in a lurch with no money at all. I owe him daddy! It's the least you can do!"

Kyle shook his head in agreement and fished the money out of his wallet and reluctantly handed it to K.C.

"Take it!" Katy demanded of K.C. "Take it or I'm not going anywhere!"

K.C. reluctantly took the money from Kyle and warily thanked him. Katy then informed her father that she wanted to speak to K.C. alone. The veins in Kyle's forehead flexed but he left the room as she requested.

"Why did you do that?" K.C. asked resisting the urge to cry again.

"Because...You're my family," Katy responded.

"I don't think I'm gonna be able to see you again before you leave...I saw my Aunt Gloria as I was gettin' off the bus...She works in this hospital."

"Did she recognize you?" Katy questioned cautiously.

"No…I don't think she got the chance," K.C. replied. "But it's too risky…I won't be able to come here again."

Katy's eyes again filled with tears as she opened her arms to K.C. "I love you," Katy whispered as they embraced.

"I love you too," K.C. cried.

"Promise me you won't spend that money on drugs," Katy pressed. "Promise me you'll take care of yourself and that you will do whatever you have to do to get better." Katy squeezed harder and her chest heaved as she made one final request of her friend, "Promise me that you're not going to die."

K.C. shook his head in agreement to all Katy's request and he let loose of his hold. As he headed for the door he turned back to Katy with a tear streaked face and a crooked smile and said, "Old Ben wanted me to give you a message…He wanted me to tell you…Jesus saves."

* * * * * * * * *

Katy couldn't sleep as she lay flat on her back staring at the ceiling and worrying about K.C.'s fate. How could she leave him at a time like this? How was he going to take care of himself? But what did she know about caring for someone in his condition. She wondered if she would be more of a hindrance than a help to him.

As the hours ticked away she was still unable to bring her mind to rest over her decision to return to Ohio with her father. Her emotions ran the gamut as she wondered why she had agreed to go back with him at all. Her innocence was gone. She was no longer the girl she once was. Not even her youthful rebellion could compare to the life she had lived on the street. Would she ever be able to tell Kyle what she'd become? She didn't know if she would be able to look at him or any other man ever again without feeling absolute revulsion and hatred of herself. Katy had been so caught up in her emotions that she hadn't noticed that someone had entered the room. She gasped in horror as she realized the shadowy figure looming over her was Sugar Man. Before she could scream Sugar Man clasped his hand over her mouth. Katy flailed her arms about trying to hit him but he managed to duck and dodge her attack until he had her completely subdued.

"My little Kat," he whispered. "Still got a lot of fight left in you don't you girl?"

Katy's eyes bulged in fear of what he had come to do to her.

"I hear you're goin' back to Ohio with *daddy*... is that right?" Sugar Man hissed. He could see by her complexion that Katy was finding it difficult to breathe so he relaxed his grip. "I'm gonna let you go but I swear to you if you scream I'll snap your neck like a twig and I'll do the same to *daddy*! Do you understand?" Katy shook her head slightly and Sugar Man slowly let go. "I just thought I'd come by and give you a little goin' away present," he said as he extracted an envelope from the inside pocket of his sport coat. He laid the package next to Katy on the bed and stood to his feet to straighten his clothes. "Open it!" he commanded.

Katy hesitantly picked up the envelope and sat up on the bed. She didn't need to open the envelope, she knew what she would find inside. The horrors of the night she had been drugged came flooding back to her.

"How do you think *daddy* would feel about getting a dozen or so of these pictures on greeting cards for the good ol' boys at his law firm?" Sugar Man smirked.

"What do you want from me?" Katy cried.

Just as Sugar Man was about to answer, the door opened again. It was Kyle. Immediately upon seeing Sugar Man he flew into a murderous rage. He lunged at him as he remembered the last time that he had attempted to challenge him. Sugar Man too remembered that encounter and flashed a sinister grin.

"If you don't get out of here right now I'm going to call hospital security and have you thrown out!" Kyle raged.

"I'll leave when I'm good and ready to leave!" Sugar Man retorted.

"Sugar Man brought me a goodbye present dad," Katy said wiping her tear-streaked face. "Wasn't that nice of him?" There was reticence in her voice as she spoke but Katy felt she had to summon the courage to beat him at his own game.

The veins in Sugar Man's fore head pulsed as Katy handed the incriminating pictures to her father. Katy stared defiantly at Sugar Man as she pressed on.

"He drugged me…He drugged me and I ended up in bed with that…disgusting creep. In fact since I left school I have been forced to sleep with a number of men…to make money, to survive, and to protect *your* reputation… I became a whore!"

Katy did not flinch as she spoke. She tried to maintain a sense of calm as her heart beat so loudly inside her chest she felt as if it were going to explode. Kyle's hands shook as he tore furiously at the pictures and threw them in Sugar Man's face. His eye's filled with tears and he sank defeated into a nearby chair. "I did this to you," he whispered.

Sugar Man swallowed hard and chuckled as he bowed his head mockingly in Katy's direction. "I gotta admit it girl," he said as he sauntered over to her bedside. "You're a lot tougher than I gave you credit for." He then leaned in and kissed her on the lips. Katy pulled away and spat at him. Angrily Sugar Man drew back his hand to hit her and Kyle leapt to her defense. He grabbed Sugar Man's arm and with the strength of youth fueled by intense fury he twisted Sugar Man's arm behind his back.

"Katy call security!" Kyle shouted.

As Katy reached for the phone Sugar Man wrestled free of Kyle's grip, brutally pushed him into the wall, and bolted out of the room.

"Daddy!" Katy screamed as she jumped out of bed.

Kyle drew up in the corner of the room like a frightened child and Katy knelt tenderly by his side and cradled him in her arms. Kyle wept and moaned in agony as he held on to what was left of his family.

26

"Choose life...Choose life...Deborah.... Choose life!"

Cookie had fallen asleep on her sofa and in her dreams she was hearing the voice of Old Ben calling after her. He called her *Deborah*. How could he know that Deborah was her real name? Why was he haunting her dreams? What was he after?

The telephone rang and broke through the fog in her mind and jarred her from her dream. She jumped up from the sofa and knocked over a glass that was sitting on her coffee table.

"H...Hello," she whispered into the receiver.

"Hey baby, it's me. Have you calmed down yet?"

Cookie immediately recognized the drawl and tensed up. She had not yet processed all the events that she'd witnessed earlier that afternoon. The accusation of murder, K.C.'s revelation that he had AIDS, and the disturbing dream that she had just been stirred from.

"Cookie, are you there?"

"What do you want?"

"I want to come and see you?"

"No...Not tonight okay. Not tonight!"

Cookie slammed down the telephone and lit a cigarette from the open pack lying on her coffee table. She got up to go to the kitchen for a towel to clean up the spill from the glass when the telephone rang again.

"What!" she screamed into the receiver.

"Mama," said the small voice on the other end.

Cookie sank down onto the sofa half-relieved and half-shocked as she recognized the voice to be that of her son Justin.

"I called to thank you for my birthday present that you sent me," Justin went on.

"I'm glad you liked it baby," Cookie choked out fighting back tears. "I'm glad you liked it."

"D'... it's Mike," came a man's voice. "I only let Justin have that present you sent him because it was delivered while I was at work. I asked you before to stop sending him stuff and I'm askin' you again. You're just confusing him. He's not givin' Val a chance to be his mother."

"I'm his mother!" Cookie shouted into the phone.

"You're a whore! You gave up your right to be his mother when you walked out on us 10 years ago. Every time he hears from you it takes me over a week to get him calmed down. Why don't you do us all a favor and leave the kid alone. Look... as long as you keep tryin' to call or write or send him things he's gonna keep thinkin' that you're comin' back. I'm makin' the best home for him that I can and Val is a good woman... She's a good mother. Why don't you just leave us alone!"

"Mike...I...Hello!...Hello!...Mike!"

The phone on the other end went dead and Cookie violently threw her end into the wall. A knock at the door gave her a start.

"Go away!" she yelled.

"Cookie it's me, K.C. I need to talk to you."

Cookie opened the door and threw herself into K.C.'s arms.

"Are you okay?" he said as he came in and closed the door behind him.

"No," she responded as she went into the kitchen to retrieve a towel. "How long have you known," she continued. "I mean about the AIDS."

"Long enough to make myself crazy," K.C. responded as he rubbed his eyes and flopped down on her loveseat. "I couldn't bring myself to tell you Cookie. I couldn't bring myself to say it out loud."

"How's Kat?" Cookie asked attempting to make polite conversation. "I've been meanin' to go by and see her...Imagine that."

"She's better," K.C. responded. "Her father's here to take her home."

"Her father?"

"Yep! It looks like somebody's finally gonna use their *"get out of hell free"* card."

Cookie leaned against the counter in her kitchen and broke down. K.C. got up from the love seat, went into the kitchen and put his arms around her to comfort her.

"I don't wanna do this any more K.C.," she cried. I just don't wanna do this any more!"

Cookie sat down on the sofa and K.C. sat facing her on the loveseat as she lit another cigarette and unburdened herself. She told him about the affair that she had with Sugar Man in St. Louis that caused her and her husband Mike to split up. She told him how her husband sued for full custody of the then two-year-old Justin and won. She also told him how she started working at a strip club as an exotic dancer because it paid better than being an office worker just to make enough money to take her husband back to court. But the dancing wasn't enough and the more of Sugar Man she had the more she had to have. He was as addictive and as alluring as any drug. She had gotten so strung out on him that she eventually followed him to Chicago and before she knew it she was prostituting herself just to make him happy.

"Do you really think he was the shooter?" Cookie questioned.

"Do you think he wasn't?" K.C. responded.

K.C.'s response sent a frightening chill throughout her entire being. Cookie knew that of all the things Sugar Man wasn't, he most certainly was capable of murder. It was more than his looks and his charisma that made him irresistible; it was the danger. As they sat together in the living room of her apartment Cookie wondered if she could get free of the insane effect he had on her or if she even wanted to.

* * * * * * * * *

It was the beginning of June and a little warmer than usual, but no one was objecting to the early arrival of summer, which was evident by the way the people were dressed. There was an abundance of cut-offs, shorts, and sandals, tee shirts, no shirts and tank tops. Everybody seemed to have cast off the restraints of winter, and spring, and were running into the summer with total abandon.

The talk in and around the neighborhood was that Sugar Man had murdered Speed and shot Katy but no substantiating proof ever came to light. No eyewitnesses ever stepped forward; their fear of Sugar Man far outweighed their trust in the police. He had even been hauled into the police station for questioning but thanks to the craftiness of Earl, his foreboding legal mouthpiece, no charges were ever brought against him. It was business as usual for him as well as all the other denizens on Madison Street.

With Katy out of the way and Cookie becoming less and less enamoured of him, Sugar Man decided to pursue other conquests. He wanted them young, naïve, and hungry. The runaways, the rebellious, the hot young teens with raging passions and hormones, the girls or boys with hurt in their eyes and wounds in their pasts. Anyone that he could manipulate or use as profit for his advantage. Those were the ones that he sought like the predator that he was.

"Hey Chris," he said to a sinewy teenaged boy as he emerged from the local grocery store. "Can I give you a ride."

Fifteen-year-old Chris Egan was a young man that Sugar Man had had his eye on for quite some time. He made several discreet inquires about him and he waited—for just the right time. Sugar Man observed that Chris had no real male influence in his life. According to what he had learned Chris never knew his father. He was the oldest of four and worked at night at McDonald's to help his mother. Sugar Man also noted that Chris was a loner. He never played much with the other kids his age. Whenever Sugar Man drove down his street he would sometimes see him sitting on the front stoop of his building drawing or just hanging out the window of his apartment with a far away look in his eyes.

The crooked little smile that Chris gave when he was offered a ride let Sugar Man know that he was ripe for the picking.

Just as Chris was about to get into Sugar Man's car the sound of a crash, and the crunch of glass and metal got Sugar Man's attention. Old Ben had angrily pushed his shopping cart into the back of Sugar Man's Mercedes.

"Have you lost your fool mind old man!" Sugar Man screamed as he jumped out of the car to survey the damage. Old Ben's shopping cart had broken a tale light and severely dented and scratched the fender.

"No more!" Old Ben responded acrimoniously. "No more children!"

The impending ruckus caused several of the stores clientele to find a spot at the window and at the door from which to catch a bird's eye view of the confrontation.

"Who's gonna pay for this!" Sugar Man demanded of Old Ben.

Rage welled up inside Old Ben as he deliberately walked toward Sugar Man to face him down. Chris, who continued to clutch his grocery bag, closed the passenger side door and backed away from the car. As he backed away he got lost in the crowd that had gathered to witness the showdown.

"You will not destroy anymore children!" Old Ben said as his gaze found Chris in the crowd.

"Destroy!" Sugar Man scoffed. "You senile old dog the only thing that is destroyed around here is my car! Look at this! Look what you did!"

The throngs of people on the street were dumbfounded as Old Ben removed a piece of wood from his cart and furiously pounded the Mercedes.

"You crazy son of a..." Sugar Man was beside himself. He pulled his switchblade from his jacket pocket and lunged toward Old Ben.

"Somebody call the police!" someone shouted as screams rang out. Old Ben dropped the piece of wood and in one uncharacteristic move grabbed Sugar Man's arm. The crowd stood ominously still, breathlessly waiting to see if Sugar Man would kill Old Ben in cold blood. The heat of the afternoon weighed down like a heavy wool coat and the buzz of the crowd was deafening, but it did not distract Old Ben or Sugar Man.

Old Ben held fast to Sugar Man's arm with both hands. Nobody knew how old Old Ben was but they were all amazed at his display of strength and agility. Perspiration formed on Sugar Man's head and rolled down the sides of his face as he tried to break free of Old Ben's grasp.

"Stick that old dude!" a gang member yelled. "Show that sorry bum who's boss!" "Yeah put us all out of *his* misery!" laughed another.

"YOU ARE CURSED MORE THAN CATTLE!" Old Ben exclaimed in a loud commanding tone. His fierce recitation quieted the taunts of his antagonists as he pressed on. "MORE THAN EVERY BEAST OF THE FIELD! ON YOUR BELLY YOU SHALL GO, AND YOU SHALL EAT DUST ALL THE DAYS OF YOUR LIFE!"

The crowd began to chuckle at Old Ben as they always had dismissing him as a doddering bible thumping indigent. They didn't realize what was happening but Sugar Man knew. This judgement had been passed once before. Those words, that tone, Sugar Man knew all too well.

"You have no power!" Old Ben continued. "Your time is up!"

The look in Old Ben's eyes let Sugar Man know that he would not win this battle. Old Ben knew that because Sugar Man could not carry out the threat to his life that the neighborhood would not see him in the same way. No one would admire him or be seduced by him or be afraid of him ever again.

The police arrived and carried Sugar Man away in handcuffs without any further incident. "Aw man you goin' out like a suckah!" one of the gang members seethed. "You let that old dude punk you! You ain't nothin'! You'a nobody!"

After what they witnessed there was no shortage of people lining up to testify against him. Even Sally, the woman who witnessed his brutal attack of Katy and subsequent shooting and murder of Speed stepped forward. Not even his oily mouthpiece was able to pull any stunts to get him out of the hell he found himself in. The court requested that Katy return to Chicago to testify. Kyle used his considerable influence to keep that from happening. He called in every favor he was owed, and it was agreed that her sworn deposition would do in lieu of her appearance. It gave Katy a great deal of satisfaction to know that Sugar Man and Earl would finally pay for their horrific crimes against her. Shortly after Sugar Man's arrest Earl Hessen found himself in over his head as well. Earl was disbarred and indicted on several counts of rape, sodomy, racketeering, and money laundering.

A grand jury found Sugar Man guilty of money laundering as well as drug trafficking, two counts of attempted murder, and murder. He was sentenced to life in prison.

27

From the time she came to Chicago Cookie had always planned to return to St. Louis to reclaim her son Justin. At the time of her divorce she didn't have enough money to hail a cab let alone pursue a custody fight. After several years of frugal spending and somewhat squalid living conditions she had finally saved enough to hire an attorney. Cookie thought that she actually had a chance to get at least joint custody, but every reputable lawyer she saw asked her the question that any judge would want to know. "Ms. Spencer, how have you been making a living since your divorce?" It was that question and her alliance with Sugar Man that Cookie knew beyond a doubt would stop her from ever getting her son back.

One after the other, every lawyer that she sought out advised her not to pursue a custody fight with her sordid background.

"I'm never gonna get my Justin back," Cookie sighed sadly as she opened the door to her meager apartment and slumped down on her sofa. As she sat defeated in the darkness of the room, she heard the creaking of the hardwood floorboards behind her. Her eyes nervously scanned the dark, and as she turned to switch on a lamp a hand grabbed her from behind. Cookie's eyes widened as she kicked and scratched at her assailant. She tried to scream but the hand that covered her mouth muffled the sound.

"Calm down!" came the menacing whisper. "Stop strugglin' and I'll let you go! I'm not gonna hurt you!"

Cookie calmed down enough to recognize the voice as that of Sugar Man. Sugar Man released his hold on her and she ran to the wall and flipped on the switch. To her amazement there he stood in his bright orange prison garb.

"Hey baby," Sugar Man whispered. "Glad to see me?"

Cookie was speechless as Sugar Man sauntered over to her. "Oooh girl I missed you somethin' awful." He reached out to caress her cheek and she turned away.

"What are you doin' here?" she said with her back to him. "You're supposed to be locked up!"

"Apparently you haven't heard the news," he said as he walked over to her and put his arm around her waist. "I escaped before they had a chance to transport me to Cook County."

Cookie squirmed uncomfortably but he held fast. "I'm not gonna hurt you girl…just relax."

Cookie was noticeably alarmed. She remembered the look in his eyes as she took the witness stand against him at his trial. She broke Sugar Man's hold on her and paced around her apartment.

"Why are you here," she demanded. "What do you want from me!"

"I'm going to Canada," he responded, "…and I want you to come with me."

"Canada!" Cookie scoffed. "And *you* want *me* to do what!"

"I need you baby," Sugar Man said pleadingly as he looked into her eyes. His charm and demeanor had worked before but Cookie was not about to allow it to work again.

"I'm not goin' anywhere with you!" Cookie raged as she violently pulled away from him.

Not to be put off Sugar Man grabbed her, wrestled her to the floor, and kissed her.

"I missed you so much girl!" he said panting heavily as he nuzzled her neck.

"Get off me!" Cookie screamed as she pushed him away with all her strength. She scrambled to the sofa and retrieved a gun from her purse. "Get out of here!" she yelled at him as she took aim.

Sugar Man arrogantly sat up and propped himself up on one arm. "What are you gonna do with that thing?" he asked as he laughed.

"I don't wanna use this!" she continued as she got to her feet. "I don't wanna have to kill you! I don't care where you go as long as you get outta here and leave me alone!"

"Baby come on now," Sugar Man pressed as he too rose to his feet. "You don't wanna kill Sugar."

"Stay back!" Cookie shouted as he moved toward her. Sugar Man froze in his tracks and raised his arms in a gesture of surrender.

"Cookie...baby," he continued. "Put the gun down before somebody gets hurt. You're not thinkin'! You don't want to shoot me! C'mon think about it... you...me...Canada! It would be a whole new life for both of us."

"Just like when I left my husband and my son and moved here, huh?" Cookie retorted.

"That was your decision to make," he replied sarcastically. "I didn't force you to leave your boy and come here with me."

"GET OUT!!!" Cookie demanded.

"O.K. girl," he said condescendingly as he put down his arms and started toward her. "Play time is over!"

"I SAID GET OUT!!!" Cookie screamed as she cocked the trigger of her .45.

Sugar Man backed down again.

"My life is a mess," Cookie cried as tears formed in her eyes. "You lied to me! I was a fool to let you talk me into this hell! Because of *you* I will never get my son back!"

"Baby I'm sorry," he responded as he put his head down in feigned sincerity. Cookie took a deep breath closed her eyes and let down her guard. As she was about to turn away Sugar Man sprang toward her and knocked her to the floor. A struggle ensued and a gunshot sounded in the silence of the room.

Sugar Man's eyes narrowed as he lay on top of Cookie and she could see the hatred and the evil in his eyes. It was as if she were seeing him for the first time. His cool and seductive veneer had been shattered, and she could finally see him for the monster he truly was. The tears in her eyes ran down the sides of her face as she lay under the weight of his body. She felt the wetness of the blood as it began to seep through her clothing. She heard the voice of Old Ben ringing in her ears. "Behold I set before you this day good and evil...Life and death...Choose life!"

With his eyes open, the dead weight of Sugar Man's frame collapsed. Cookie squeezed her eyes shut and gasped for air. With the gun still wedged between them Cookie tried to free herself from underneath his body.

After what seemed like an eternity, Cookie was finally able to roll Sugar Man's body off hers. Her hands, her clothes, everything was covered with blood. Cookie moved into a corner of the room, pulled her knees in to her chest and waited.

* * * * * * * * * *

October was approaching and there was a decidedly wintry chill blowing off Lake Michigan throughout the annals of the city. News of Sugar Man's demise had resounded across the country. Cookie's face was plastered on newspapers and television programs from coast to coast. Because Sugar Man was considered an armed and dangerous felon his death was ruled self defense. No charges were brought against Cookie. When the publicity waned she decided to leave Chicago and move back to St. Louis. She begged K.C. to come with her but he would not hear of it.

"I'll miss you baby," Cookie whimpered as she held tightly onto her friend inside the bus terminal.

"You can always come back for my funeral," K.C. cracked.

"Don't do that," Cookie begged as she released him and wiped her face.

K.C. looked at her realizing that he had joked about his condition once too often, and to the people that really loved him it was no laughing matter.

"You're gonna get your son back," K.C. said supportively. "I know you will." Cookie smiled wryly and shook her head in agreement. "Here!" K.C. announced as he pulled a crudely wrapped rectangular package from the inside of his coat. "It's a going away present," he continued proudly.

"K.C. you shouldn't have done this...You..."

"Shhhh," K.C. said as he gave her one last hug. "You've got a life to start livin' and you've got a bus to catch."

The tears flowed again as Cookie choked out the words; "I love you baby boy."

"I love you too!" K.C. responded trying to sound cheerful. "Now go!...Justin's waitin' for you!"

Cookie turned and grabbed her carry on bag and ran through the door leading out to the bus. K.C. stood at the bus station window and pressed his hands to the glass waiting for Cookie to settle in her seat. She found a window seat and looked out to find her friend. Minutes later the bus began to pull away and Cookie waved her final farewell. Unable to hold back any longer a single tear streamed down the side of K.C.'s face as he watched the bus disappear up the road.

A million memories flooded his mind as he stood there at the window. But one memory stood out above them all, the day that fate brought him to Chicago, to that very bus terminal, and to Drake Sommersbee. After several minutes K.C. turned away from the window, wiped his face with the back of his hand and headed out into the chilly autumn night air.

* * * * * * * * *

Cookie sat on the bus and smiled as she gently opened the gift-wrapped package K.C. had given her. *"When God Doesn't Make Sense,"* she read aloud as she ran her hand over the cover of the book. She opened the inside cover to read, *"Cookie this is how my journey started...Love always, K.C."* Cookie closed her eyes and laid her head back as she held the book close to her chest and cried.

* * * * * * * * *

K.C., with the help of a social worker, was now being supported by the various agencies in Chicago that assisted HIV and AIDS patients recovering from alcohol and drug addictions. At its worst the disease had ravaged K.C.'s physical appearance so dramatically that he was barely recognizable. After recovering from a bout with pneumonia he was released from the hospital as his death vigil continued. How he'd wished that fate had been so kind as to take him as quickly as it took Drake. He found that his acceptance into the "fellowship of the damned" was in stark contrast to those that knew him in and around his old neighborhood. Most of those who used to party with him and get high with him were now turning away from him whether out of fear, pity, or ignorance. The only one that seemed to treat him as if he were still the same old K.C. was Popps who owned the liquor store down the street from the apartment he used to share with Katy. K.C. often found himself taking the bus back to his old digs just to have a conversation with Popps, or play chess, or backgammon, or just to feel normal again.

Had he been thinking K.C. would have realized that it was Sunday and the liquor store was closed on Sundays. He had obviously not thought about that, and as he got off the bus and headed across the street it dawned on him.

"Aw man!" he said in exasperation.

It seemed to be getting colder as he turned and headed up the street, as if instinctively he were headed home. Back to the apartment where he used to live. As he reached the building he stopped just short of the alley near where Speed was killed. He leaned against the brick and pulled two photos from his tattered wallet. The edges of the pictures were frayed and they were torn but he could still make out the images. One was of him and Drake two Christmases before he died and the other was of he, Katy, and Cookie inside Gemini's at his 21st birthday party. He laughed to himself as he recalled all the fun he and his friends had that night.

"K.C...K.C. is that you?"

K.C.'s heart seemed to skip a beat as he heard the voice. "Kat," he whispered as he slowly lifted his head to see. "Kat...Is that you?" he said in disbelief focusing on the shadowy figure approaching him.

"Yes it's me," she replied.

K.C. beamed despite himself as Katy stepped out from the shadows. There she stood dressed in the old sweatshirt he had given her, a pair of jeans, tennis shoes, and a big wool coat with her hair pulled back and tied. K.C. thought to himself that despite what she had gone through over the past year Katy seemed innocent and untouched by her experiences. Katy opened her arms and started to run toward K.C. but he turned away from her.

"Kat don't!" he yelled abruptly.

"K.C. what's the matter," Katy asked confused at his reaction. "Aren't you glad to see me?"

K.C. kept his face toward the wall as he answered her. He was thrilled to see her again, he just didn't want her to see him.

"K.C. I didn't come all the way back here from Ohio to talk to the wall," she chided. "Please...Look at me."

"I...I can't."

"K.C...It's O.K. Whatever it is... It's O.K. You're my friend. I love you."

K.C.'s excitement over seeing Katy again was short lived. He was soon overcome with feelings of shame and embarrassment. He pulled the collar of his jacket up around his ears and pulled his cap down further on his head.

"You don't have to hide from me," Katy said sympathetically. "I'm not afraid of you. I love you."

Katy walked closer to him and put her arms around him from behind and embraced him. "I love you," she repeated.

K.C. let down his defenses as tears streamed down his gaunt face. It felt good to have someone embrace him again. It felt good to have human contact from someone who wasn't afraid of him. He knew that like Cookie, Katy truly loved him. No matter the circumstances that brought them together the three of them found something in each other that they never really had or may have had and taken for granted. In that one small word that is so often abused and misused came the comfort and strength that he needed. K.C. turned and wept in her arms.

The two of them walked across the street to the park where they had spent so many nights sitting, talking, and sharing with each other.

"You look so different," K.C. said.

"I am different," Katy gleefully responded. "My whole life is different! I've found GOD. Not the GOD that makes you turn your nose up at people that are different, or the GOD that tells you that everybody has to be like you or do things in the way you do them to be *saved*. I found the GOD that embodies love, peace, freedom, compassion, forgiveness and that's just the beginning. He's doing something for me that being out on the street never could have done. *He's* making me whole!"

"GOD?" K.C. inquired earnestly.

"When I moved back to Ohio," Katy continued. "I found the best church! I found a bunch of people that don't condemn me or label me...they accept me."

"Acceptance," K.C. scoffed. "What's that like?"

"It's a wonderful feeling," Katy gushed as she stood up and spun around like a giddy schoolgirl. "Just to know that people can genuinely care about you without having a hidden agenda. They don't care what I was! To them I'm not a whore...I'm a child of GOD! I'm a long way from being completely whole, but I'm a lot closer than I used to be. And for the first time in my life, I have hope."

"HOPE ain't nothin' but a four letter word," K.C. said as he turned away from her again.

Not to be put off Katy pulled on his shoulder to turn him back to her. "I got another word for you," she continued. *"Restoration!"*

K.C. put his hand up to brush her away as he stood up. "I'm dying! Can't you see that! I've gone too far! I've done too much, and now I'm payin' for it! Nobody wants to have nothin' to do with a tired old fag!"

"You want to know what I've learned K.C.," Katy pressed. "GOD hates the sin...but He loves the sinner. It doesn't matter what people say. You are not a "fag" in GOD's eyes...You are His child and He loves you. He loved you so much He died for you...He's real K.C. and He's not far away...all you've got to do is talk to Him."

Suddenly a brilliant light flashed across the night sky and rested between the two buildings across the street from where K.C. and Katy stood. It was so bright that it illuminated the entire street and made it appear as if it were broad daylight even though it was not. All activity on the street came to a halt in its wake. Despite it's blinding yet dazzling brilliance Katy was drawn to it. She fell to her knees in acknowledgement of the presence of GOD.

K.C. looked at Katy as if she had lost her mind. There was nothing there he thought to himself as he shielded his eyes. The truth was there to see, although K.C. couldn't see it, Katy saw it all too well. He covered his face with his jacket.

"K.C. look at Him!" she begged. "Look...and live!"

At her request K.C. uncovered his eyes and tried to look into the light but it was too overwhelming.

"Amazing grace," Katy began in a soft singsong voice. "How sweet the sound that saved a wretch like me...I once was lost but now...I'm found...Was blind...but now...I ...see."

The Glory of the Lord hovered over the entire street as the next sound that K.C. heard drew him from his hiding place. It was the voice, he thought, of Old Ben.

"GREATER LOVE HATH NO MAN THAN TO LAY DOWN HIS LIFE FOR A FRIEND...FOR ALL HAVE SINNED AND COME SHORT OF THE GLORY OF GOD BUT GOD COMMENDED HIS LOVE TOWARD US, IN THAT, WHILE WE WERE YET SINNERS CHRIST DIED FOR US...FOR GOD SO LOVED THE WORLD THAT HE GAVE HIS ONLY BEGOTTEN SON THAT WHOSOEVER BELIEVES IN HIM SHALL NOT PERISH BUT HAVE EVERLASTING LIFE."

For the first time K.C.'s eyes were opened. Not his physical eyes but the eyes of his understanding. The words that he heard touched him in a place that no man had ever reached.

"K.C.," said GOD. "My son... WILL YOU BE MADE WHOLE?"

"*Son*," K.C. thought to himself. "GOD... GOD called me *son*. He didn't call me punk, or sissy, or homo, or fag...He called me *son*."

There were no labels. There were no barriers. The voice of GOD was the sweetest, clearest sound that K.C. had ever heard. All he had left to do was repent. K.C. fell to his knees in surrender. He surrendered the pain, the loss, and his soul to the GOD that knew him as a *son*. In that moment of surrender K.C. had an epiphany. He opened in eyes, he opened his heart, he opened his mouth, and he said *"Yes Lord."*

THE TESTIMONY

I murdered a man and ran away. I was a borderline alcoholic. I was a drug addict and I slept with men...lots of men, for money and for pleasure. Can you honestly say that if someone like me walked into your church and sat next to you all you'd feel is the love of GOD? If you can't maybe you're not as ready as you think you are.

It seemed like I'd lived a thousand lifetimes in just 23 years. Some of the things that happened to me I asked for, and some I didn't. I never knew anything about GOD growing up. I did know a lot about pain. My mama didn't go to church and she never made me go either. As far as I was concerned there was no GOD, at least not one that I could see. I guess it took me comin' to Chicago and loosin' everything to let me know that you don't necessarily have to see GOD with your natural eyes. It's like Elizabeth Goldberg said *GOD is sovereign and He can do what HE wants to do when HE wants to do it.* We can't choose who our parents are. We can't choose our destiny. GOD didn't create us for that. HE created us for Himself, to love everybody and to love Him. Isn't that what we all want anyway just knowin' that somebody loves us unconditionally. I know that now.

I'm not proud of who I was, or what I did, and that's one of the things that kept me away from people who think they got it all together. Church people. Religious people. "How can we hear without a preacher?" Since you don't want us in your church are you gonna come out here and get us? Can you accept us? Can you love us?

I never knew why I grew up like I did. It didn't make sense. Even after I let GOD into my heart it didn't make sense. My body was still dying. I even had some of the same desires and urges that I had when I was in the street. It wasn't until I started hangin' out with Chris Eagan that things really started to come together. Chris wasn't much older than I was when I started out and he was gay. *Gay,* what a stupid word, what's so gay about any of this.

Chris and me started to develop a relationship of sorts before I admitted to anybody that I was sick. I know what you're probably thinkin'; there was nothin' sexual between us. We were just friends. See, I think that's what's wrong with the world, people think that if you're gay you want to sleep with every man you come in contact with, or put some kind of spell on them so they can be gay too. I mean, how stupid is that? Anyway, Chris was just a confused kid tryin' to find a place in the world. He just wanted to be accepted. And I didn't want him to end up feelin' like he had no choices. I didn't want him to end up killin' his self because nobody understood him. Or tryin' to find love by confusin' it with sex. It's funny I think I actually ended up tellin' him about GOD's love. And how GOD loved him and GOD wanted to care about him. Kat said I was *witnessing.* Imagine that...me... a witness.

Chris was an artist and he had a lot of potential. How was anybody ever gonna know what kind of a man *he could be* if they labeled him before they got a chance to know him. We used to talk for hours on the front step of his building. He showed me some of his artwork. He had drawn pictures of me and Kat and Cookie, Speed, Tee and even Old Ben. I'd have to say the kid was pretty good.

After a while my eyes started botherin' me so he would even read the bible to me. Before I knew it there were a couple of other guys that joined us.

Kat was there too. It seems that livin' back at home with her father turned out not to be such a good idea after all. She found out that her mother had left her a small fortune after she died that she was suppose to get on her 21st birthday, a little somethin' that her father forgot to tell her about. If she hadn't been in such a hurry to get back to Chicago after the funeral she might have found out on her own. Kyle did his best to keep her from findin' out but she did anyway. Secrets always have a way of comin' out. Anyway, Kat would gather us all up and we'd sing and we'd pray and we'd read the bible to each other. . .We were the Church of the Lost Souls. We banded together to comfort each other because each other was all we had, well, each other and GOD.

I wish I could start over again. I'd do it different this time. I'd see *the light* a lot sooner. Isn't that what you're supposed to say when your time is almost up and you don't have any more chances left? GOD gave His love to us freely while we were undeserving, filthy, shameful, prideful, lustful, rebellious, unloving sinners. Jesus Christ died for *you and me so* that one day we could live again and none of the things we experience in life can outlast eternity. Don't wait! You may not be like me, or Kat, Cookie, or Tee but there is something in you that is not like GOD. I hope you get it together before it's too late.

Before I go I'd like to share with you one of my favorite scriptures ... *I want you to know, brethren, that the things which happened to me have actually turned out for the furtherance of the gospel. Philippians 1:12*

If you run into Chris... just ask him.

KEITH PATRICK COLEMAN
(K.C.)
1975- 1998

FINAL THOUGHTS

Have you ever wondered what kind of destiny had been missed in that homeless man or woman you pass on the street as you go about your busy lives?

Have you ever thought about the horrors in a man's life that might cause him to seek comfort or some semblance of love with another man?

Have you ever considered what kind of indignities the prostitute suffers daily as her body is being enslaved and sold to the highest bidder? Yet we look down on her and say, "I could never do that."

Can you imagine the traumatic events in a person's life that would cause them to crave the escape of a crack pipe?

Have you ever used words like slut, tramp, bum, dope head, or faggot? What kind of words do you think GOD uses to describe us?

Ephesians 6:12 Tells us that... *we wrestle not against flesh and blood, but against principalities, against powers, against the rulers of darkness of this age, against spiritual hosts of wickedness in high places.*

Demonic forces are what lurk behind the walls of a person's internal struggle. Sugar Man embodied the evil that we all abhor, and some are powerless to control. The devil wants to isolate us so that he can control us. As in Katy's situation she discovered that the devil did not just want to posses her soul, he wanted to literally kill her. And that's exactly what he wants to do to all of us.

If not for the grace of GOD we all could have died in our sin. But how do the undesirables get the message.

In the Hebrew, Benjamin means, son of my right hand, the right hand of GOD. Old Ben symbolized the messenger, the deliver, but GOD commissioned the Christian for the job. *You go out into the highways and hedges, and compel them to come in, that my house may be filled. Luke 14:23*

Restoration is for everybody, no matter how perverse we as Christians believe him or her to be. We are all *cracked pots* yet GOD chooses to love us and use us in spite of. *For GOD so loved the world, that He gave...John 3:16* We were all saved from something.

K.C. believed that he too was beyond salvation but when he came to understand that GOD loved him in spite of the labels that were attached to him, he was able to accept the unfathomable mercy of GOD. *The wages of sin is death...* K.C. had done wrong in his life and had for the most part gone unpunished, but he found out that ....*the gift of GOD is eternal life. Romans 6:23*

If you find yourself in a situation of shame or guilt don't be thrown by what the people say, they have neither a heaven or a hell to put you in. GOD is a GOD of forgiveness. *When the fullness of time had come, GOD sent forth His Son, born of a woman, born under the law to redeem those who were under the law, that we might receive the adoption of sons. And because you are sons, GOD has sent forth the Spirit of His Son into your hearts, crying out, "Abba Father!" Therefore you are no longer a slave but a son, and if a son, then an heir of GOD through Christ. Galatians 4: 4-7*

Don't wait! "Wouldn't you rather be with a GOD that can satisfy you for an eternity than to be with a man that can only satisfy you for a night?" Old Ben.

For information about *Will You Be Made Whole?* or *Restoration* the stage play or *Restoration* the book please write to:

ayala_writer2000@yahoo.com
www.geocities.com/jehovahjireh_ayala

In the beginning was the word ...

Before I formed you in the womb, I knew you ... Jeremiah 1:5

WILL YOU BE MADE WHOLE is Eric's highly anticipated follow-up work to the inspirational story of RESTORATION. Eric was born in Chicago, Illinois, reared and educated in Indianapolis, Indiana, and presently resides in Atlanta, Georgia where he is an active member of Total Grace Christian Center in Decatur, Georgia. He is currently working on his third novel as well as writing and directing for the stage.

"Talent can only get you so far. It is the anointing that breaks yokes. I pray that you have been provoked to change."